FAST FORWARD

an Alt Er Love novella

XIO AXELROD

XIO AXELROD

ISBN: 978-0-9989316-2-3

This one is for the SKAMily, (especially the SKAM Elders: Lizzie, Camilla, KT, Monique, Freya, Allie, and Carrie). As well as for Sofia, Matti, and everyone at SKAM Stories, and Magni Onsoien for her input on the Norwegian. We all met under one big, beautiful umbrella.
Remember... Alt er love!

A bit of Norwegian

Faen ~ *Fuck or damn, depending on the context*
    Fy faen ~ *Fucking hell (or holy shit)*
    Jeg ~ *I*
    Deg ~ *You*
    Du er jævla deilig ~ *You are so fucking hot.*
    and, of course,
    Jeg elsker deg ~ *I love you*

Chapter 1

Ian Waters hated parties. Hated the smell of them, beer-breath clouds and stale nachos. Cheap perfume and sweat. He hated the sound of music pouring out of shitty speakers, hated the abnormally raised voices and the pathetic attempts at small talk.

He wasn't a people person, and he sure as shit wasn't a party person.

But he'd made a promise to his friend Siv, and Ian was a man of his word. Or tried to be.

When a drunk, giggly brunette fell into him, buffeted by the writhing bodies on the makeshift dance floor in Siv's living room, Ian's only thought was to get the hell out of there as soon as possible.

"Oh my God, I'm so sorry!" The girl screeched into his ear, nearly deafening him. She flipped her dark brown hair over her shoulder and gaped at him.

The music wasn't *that* loud. Her volume was entirely unnecessary. It was also completely unnecessary for her to lean on him so heavily, her fingers gripping his biceps like she thought a chasm had opened up behind her and feared her imminent death.

Through his mind's lens, Ian pictured a wide-shot of the Persian rug as it transformed into a canyon, saw the brunette perched on the precipice with fear in her eyes.

Or maybe it was the edge of a skyscraper overlooking downtown Philadelphia. A helicopter hovering just off the edge of the roof, with a sniper's gun trained on them both.

But would she be the victim or the villain?

"Hey!"

Ian blinked, plummeting back into his reality. The party. The clingy woman.

"Uh…what?"

She looked at him like he was a few eggs short of a dozen. "I said, I've seen you before. I think we met at Dirty Frank's?"

No way in hell. He shrugged. "Sorry."

Her grip on his arms turned into something like a caress, and Ian recoiled. Inwardly. Outwardly, he remained stiff as a board.

She was attractive enough, with shiny, bouncy, shampoo commercial-worthy hair that fell past her shoulders.

The girl reminded him of that actress from *That 70s Show*. Mila Kunis. A slightly alien quality to her features that would look amazing on 8mm film.

Mila's voice was smoky, a little naughty. She was petite, but still a little curvy. Feminine but boyish. If that did it for him, Mila would do it for him.

Clingy-Mila's lookalike did not have the smoky voice. Or maybe she did, he couldn't tell, what with the yelling over the nineties hip-hop and all.

"Are you even listening to me?"

Ah. And now was annoyed. No point in playing nice, then.

"Not really, no."

She frowned and finally – finally – let Ian go.

"Wow. You're kind of a dick!"

Her scowl transformed her features from attractive-for-a-chick to banshee.

Ian almost laughed at the look of pure disgust on her face but decided it wouldn't earn him any Brownie points. He also tried to hide his relief when she turned and walked away, bouncing back into the heaving mass of bodies.

Siv threw great parties. Everyone said so.

Ian didn't understand the appeal.

Glancing at his smartphone, he realized he'd been there for forty-five minutes. Surely that was long enough to be considered a proper guest. Long enough that leaving wouldn't seem weird, right? Wouldn't garner those pitying looks, inevitably followed by pleas for him to stay a little longer?

"There you are!" Siv, lovely Siv, brushed past a clump of people and grabbed his arm. "I've been looking everywhere for you."

"Oh, I, uh, I was talking to someone, but I should get going."

Siv's face fell. "Ian…"

She didn't need to say more, Ian knew that look. He knew her so well. Siv was the closest thing to family he'd ever had, though she'd started out as just an acquaintance. Somewhere along the way she'd gotten under his skin.

He hated to disappoint her, no matter how lightly.

"Won't you stay a while? I made the shrimp salad you love, and…" Her gaze darted toward the other side of the room before meeting his again. She had the loveliest green eyes. Like an Irish meadow. "There's someone I want you to meet."

Sigh.

Ian gazed longingly at the door. If only he hadn't been trapped by fake-Mila.

"Sure," he said, forcing a smile. "Lead the way."

Her smile was radiant. Siv grabbed his hand and pulled with far more strength than he'd given her credit for. It was all Ian could do not to trip over his size thirteen feet.

Heads turned as they passed. Ian wasn't naïve enough not to know why. He was a kind of celebrity in their circles. The former wunderkind of their academic world, though he hadn't been a teen in years.

After graduating high school at thirteen, and getting his bachelor's at seventeen, Ian was three years post-doctorate and well into his career as a professor of Theoretical Physics at the University of

Philadelphia. The youngest ever to be on the fast track toward tenure.

The novelty of the "baby professor" had worn off long ago, but there were some who still whispered when he walked into the room. *There he is, the kid who could have had everything.*

He ignored them per usual, dutifully following Siv into whatever socially awkward situation she would have him ascribe to. It was Siv, and Ian found he'd do just anything for her.

Almost anything, it turned out, because she led him straight into the fires of hell. Or rather, straight to the last person he ever thought he'd see again.

Ian's step faltered along with his breath. He couldn't do this. Not again. Not now, when he'd finally gotten his shit together.

Jessen Sørensen.

At six feet and nearly five inches, Jessen towered over everyone, including Ian. And Ian was usually the tallest person in the room.

Hair piled high atop his head in ridiculous, gravity-defying waves, Jessen held court in the corner of the room. All effortless smiles, and flashing blue eyes. No one could draw a crowd like him. He didn't even need to do anything, just breathe. Breathe and smile and be Jessen. Beautiful, wild, unattainable Jessen.

"You okay?" Concern in her voice, Siv turned to face him, her hand still in his.

He'd squeezed hers a bit too hard and eased his grip. "Yeah. Fine. Sorry."

He was not fine. He was three yards away from becoming a shivering, quivering mess.

Jessen fucking Sørensen.

"Come on, I want you to meet this guy. He's an ex-pat from Norway, like me. You'll like him!"

God, she looked so eager. Eyes bright, beaming up at him like she was about to watch him unwrap a gift.

Ian nodded and willed his feet to move.

They passed the front door, and he thought about making a break for it.

Jessen hadn't spotted him yet.

Maybe he could feign illness and slip away. He was a little light-headed, after all. Nauseous. Short of breath. Maybe he really was sick.

They stopped, and Ian went into panic mode. Jessen's voice – his motherfucking voice – surrounded him. Filled him.

Fuck.

"That's insane!" The guy to the left of him exclaimed, utterly impressed by whatever yarn Jessen had spun. He probably had reams of them, stories from his days on the road with his twin brother the rock god.

Shit. Ian couldn't do this. He was just about to make his excuses and take his leave when it happened.

"Hey, Jess, this is the guy I told you about." Siv yanked Ian forward until he stood toe-to-toe with the subject of every dream he'd had for the last seven years, and more than a few of his nightmares.

Jessen was smiling when he met his gaze. To his credit, the smile only wavered for a millisecond before he dialed up the brightness and extended his hand.

To Ian.

Like he'd never seen him before.

"Nice to meet you, man, I'm Jess."

Well, fuck.

Chapter 2

The hand was warm, a little more calloused than Ian remembered. And boy, did he remember. Those fingers had turned him inside out. Had made him and then broken him, again and again.

"Hi." It was little more than a croak, but Ian mentally patted himself on the back for managing it.

Jessen's eyes, those glacial blue eyes, held his gaze for longer than necessary.

Was he trying to place him? Had some memory dislodged itself from his no doubt extensive catalog of conquests? If so, he didn't show it. Merely nodded and turned his attention back to those gathered.

Ian kept as still as he could. As quiet as death. He tried to follow the thread of the conversation, something about a new venue that opened in Philly.

"It's gorgeous, the acoustics are perfect," said a mahogany-skinned pixie across the circle from him. "You should tell your brother to do a surprise show there or something. Everyone would go nuts."

Jessen nodded, smiling The Smile. The fake one he reserved for his brother's acolytes.

Ian hated that he knew Jessen well enough to recognize it, while the man seemingly had no recollection of him at all.

"Mattias is on tour now, isn't he?"

This came from a plaid-clad hipster with the most manicured beard Ian had ever seen. The guy's pants were so tight, Ian could see the outline of his iPhone. And he wore suspenders. Red ones that matched neither the green in his shirt nor the olive in his jeans. And since his pants were painted on, it meant he wore them ironically.

Ian rolled his eyes.

Jessen's gaze flicked to his face, and the corner of his mouth twitched. "Yeah, he's down south somewhere. Atlanta, I think."

"Why aren't you with him?"

"I don't always tour with him," Jessen said with only a bit of an edge. "I have my own thing going on."

"Oh," hipster-dude nodded, eyeing Jessen with a patronizing grin. "Right. I forgot."

Ouch.

The instinct to defend Jessen rose out of nowhere. Before Ian knew it, the words had tumbled from his mouth.

"Personally, I like Jessen's music better than his brother's."

All eyes turned to Ian.

The sly smile on Siv's lips told him just how much he had stepped in it. Now he'd have to confess to knowing who Jessen was, while still feigning ignorance about just how well he knew the man himself.

Because Ian knew him, every ivory-skinned inch of him. From the silken strands that brushed his forehead, to the smooth expanse of his belly, to the eight inches between his legs, Ian knew him.

He knew the frenetic energy of his fingers when they held an instrument. He knew the ragged moan he made when he was in the throes of pleasure. He knew the deafening silence of being left behind by Jessen Sørensen.

The ache. The hollowness.

Ian cleared his throat. "Only my opinion."

"I didn't know you were a fan," Siv said, smirking up at him.

"I wouldn't say I'm a fan."

"What would you say, then?" Jessen's voice was huskier than even Ian had remembered.

Ian refused to meet his gaze, which he knew would be trained on him. Whether Jessen had any memory of their time together or not, he could never pass up the opportunity to hear praise for his music.

"I…" Ian searched Siv's gleaming, oak floorboards for the right words. "In comparison, I prefer your style of music over Matt's." He chanced a look, only to find Jessen practically beaming at him.

God, the man was…

Beautiful wasn't the word.

He'd been all angles and sharp edges seven years ago when they were both teetering on the brink of adulthood, both thrust into a world they hadn't been ready for. For Ian, it was academia. For Jessen, it had been his brother's superstardom.

Ian had met Jess after one of his and Matt's on-campus concerts, having been assigned to document the event for his film studies class, his favorite elective. He'd gotten a lot of fantastic footage that night.

But Ian had lost himself not in the music or the imagery, but in the angelic guitarist standing just outside the spotlight his brother had occupied. He hadn't been able to take his eyes off him.

Ian had known, long before then, that'd he was attracted to men, though he had never really acted on it. Hadn't even ever been with a woman outside of a few drunken kisses at parties. But Ian had never felt the magnetic pull, the inexorable attraction to another human being that he'd felt the night he met Jessen Sørensen.

It was there again tonight as Jessen leveled that piercing, teasing gaze on him.

It took a few seconds to realize Jessen hadn't responded, only stared at him with laughter in his eyes. Laughter and interest. The silence stretched on for an eternity, or maybe it was only a few seconds.

"Meh," hipster-dude muttered. "No offense, your stuff is good, but your brother is a whole different level. There's an existential quality to his music that only comes along once in a generation."

Jessen laughed. It was a full-throated, joyous sound that punched the air out of Ian's lungs.

He loved Jessen's laugh. Had missed it. It was like hearing a favorite song from long ago.

"*Faen*, my brother would kick you in the balls if he heard you say that," Jessen said once he'd settled down. "Sex, drugs, and rock-n-roll, it's all he lives for. Any philosophizing you hear in his songs is totally accidental."

Or it's from you, Ian thought, knowing Jessen wrote more than half of Matt's first album, though he wasn't credited. He wanted to speak up again, reveal that particular truth, when Jessen spoke again.

"People see what they want to see," he said to no one in particular, swirling the bottle in his hand in slow circles in front of him. "You can paint the picture, but they'll interpret it any way they like."

Jessen cocked his head at hipster-dude. "You present yourself as an intellectual, while the opposite may be true. You might be a sheeple, blindly following a trend. Plaid shirt, pompadour, prescription glasses you don't actually need."

Hipster-dude flinched, his mouth twisting.

Jessen turned up the wattage on his smile. "Don't fret, it's just an example. Not talking about you, per se."

Yes, you are.

As if he heard Ian's thought, Jessen turned to him and winked before addressing hipster-dude again.

The room was suddenly hot. Ian needed to leave. Now.

"Have you been holding out on me?" Siv whispered, tugging on the rolled-up sleeve of his button-down shirt. "How do you have secret signals with someone I just introduced you to?"

"Secret signals?" He bent closer, terrified Jessen would overhear.

"You know his music."

"So? A lot of people do."

Siv leaned back, eyeing him.

Ian tried to will the blood away from his cheeks. They were hot, and he knew he was likely tomato red.

Siv took his hand and pulled him away from the circle. "Are you okay? You don't look so good."

She placed the back of her hand on his forehead.

"Shit, Ian. You're burning up!"

Ian smiled what he hoped was a reassuring smile and gently removed her hand.

"I'm all right, Siv. Really."

She squinted as she reached up and ran her fingers through his thick, unruly hair.

It felt amazing, and he closed his eyes, leaning into her touch for a second.

"Are you sure?" The concern in her voice touched him far too deeply. Really, she was the only one who gave a good goddamn about him.

Ian opened his eyes and pulled Siv into a hug, dropping his head to her shoulder. It was a stretch. He had a good five inches of height on her.

"Absolutely sure." He released her and stood up straight. "I'm just tired. I have a shit ton of papers to grade, still, not to mention final projects to watch. Probably sixty hours' worth."

Siv winced. "*Faen.*"

He chuckled. "Yeah, fuck is right."

A warm, soft hand landed on either side of his face, and he peered down into her green eyes.

"Take care of yourself, okay? Go home and relax for the night. The work will be there tomorrow. You've got time."

As the Assistant Department Chair, Siv was an ideal boss for Ian. Barely thirty years old and not yet jaded, she was as passionate about teaching as he was, and as dedicated to the students, but she also believed in having a life. Hers was full of family and friends, and Ian envied that. Envied having a network of support.

He was on his own.

"Oh, shit, I know that look." Siv pulled him into another hug, wrapping him up tight in her freakishly long arms and rubbing circles on his back as if he were an infant.

He loved it.

"You are not alone, baby brother. What's Siv's is yours."

"I hate when you call me that," he protested weakly.

"No you don't," she replied, teasing him.

She was right. If he had a sister, it was Siv Bergdahl.

Ian held her, rocking them for a bit and relishing in the contact. When he stood, ready to take his leave of her and of the party, he felt eyes on him. He turned and his gaze snagged on Jessen's.

His expression was inscrutable, but it made Ian pull away from Siv with something like guilt in his gut.

Jessen's eyes narrowed, and then he turned back to the group.

Geez. Ian's stomach did a backflip.

"Okay, I'm just gonna grab my jacket and make my escape."

"Okay. Call me tomorrow," Siv replied, already returning to the revelers. Ian wasn't even sure what they were celebrating.

He wound his way through the party and slipped through to the kitchen, grateful to find it deserted. Empty beer bottles littered every flat surface, and Ian groaned. Siv would have to clean this up all by herself, and he'd feel guilty for letting her.

Rolling up his sleeves a bit further, he tackled the kitchen table first, emptying the liquids into the sink and tossing the glass bottles and aluminum cans into the recycling bin. He'd just cleared one side of the countertop when the door opened and closed behind him.

"Before you get on my case for helping, I wasn't about to leave this mess for you to clean up on your own."

"You always were so thoughtful, Ian."

That fucking voice. It hit Ian's bloodstream like a shot of vodka. He dropped the bottle in his hand. It clattered into the sink but thankfully didn't break. He couldn't say the same about his nerves. They were fried.

His hands shook, so he grabbed the edge of the counter. Ian couldn't find the strength to turn around and face him.

"Sorry if I startled you," Jessen said, his voice closer.

Ian swallowed past the scream in his throat. He wanted to run. He wanted to run so fucking bad.

"Not even going to look at me?"

Knees shaking, heart pounding, and palms sweating, though it could have been the dishwater, Ian turned. He kept a firm grip on the counter because it might have been the only thing holding him up.

Jessen Sørensen was only five feet away. It may as well have been a mile.

"Hey." The blond exhaled a shaky breath. He seemed almost shy, his voice barely above a whisper. "I couldn't believe it was you, I can't…"

Ian frowned. This was not the Jessen he remembered, flighty and aloof and sexy as fuck.

Okay, he was still sexy as fuck. If anything, he'd gotten hotter which was off the Richter scale of unfairness, as he was already a benchmark ten all those years ago.

"Your hair is a little darker," Jessen said, a soft smile curving his edible mouth.

"I'm older," Ian replied.

Jessen nodded, his gaze drinking him in.

Ian remembered what it used to do to him, his expression. Remembered how quickly it could get him to drop to his knees.

"And wiser," Ian added belatedly.

Jessen's gaze flicked up to his, filled with caution. Good.

"What are you doing in Philadelphia?"

Jessen exhaled and leaned against the kitchen table. "I live here now."

"What?" The word popped out of Ian's mouth before he could stop it.

Ignoring the panic in Ian's voice, Jessen nodded as he traced the wood grain of the table with his fingers.

"Yep. I'm officially a Philly luddite."

Ian opened his mouth to say *fuck you* when he noticed the grin tugging at the corner of Jessen's mouth.

He remembered.

He remembered how defensive Ian was about his hometown, and how eagerly he'd roll up his sleeves to defend it.

It had been in Jessen's bag of tricks to taunt him with insults about Philadelphia, get him riled up, and then fuck the resentment out of him.

Ian's skin heated. "What are you looking at?"

Jessen smirked. Asshole. "How have you been?"

"Why do you care?"

Jessen's face fell just a little bit and Ian mentally high-fived himself.

When he spoke again, his voice had softened to a caress. "Ian, why wouldn't I care how you were?"

"You haven't cared in the last seven years."

Jessen nodded. "I can see why you might think so but, *faen*…of course I care. You're the one who got away."

Chapter 3

Ian melted, just a little, before his brain rebooted. Whatever game Jessen was about, Ian was not going to play.

"The one who got away? You mean the one who escaped."

Jessen's smile was lethal. "That implies some sort of danger. Were you in danger, baby?"

He glided across the floor on his too-long legs, like some human giraffe, barely disturbing the air molecules in the room. So fucking smooth was Jessen Sørensen. Ian hated him a little.

Not enough, apparently, because he didn't move.

He didn't move when Jessen stopped in front of him. Didn't move when he reached up and brushed the hair out of his eyes, his pinky dragging across Ian's forehead with the lightest touch. He didn't move as Jessen crowded him against the sink, hovering but not touching.

Ian managed not to sigh at Jessen's soft exhalation. "*Faen*, I forgot how fucking beautiful you really are."

But he had to close his eyes, because what? The? Fuck?

"You cannot be serious."

"Oh, I am very serious, young Ian."

Ian's eyes snapped open. "Don't call me that, I'm not a kid

anymore. Neither of us is a kid anymore."

Jessen's gaze dragged down Ian's body, and it was too close to a caress. "No," he rasped. "You are not a kid anymore."

"You haven't changed, though."

It was a lie. Jessen had changed. Time had carved into the raw, natural beauty of the boy and turned him into a well-aged museum piece. Michelangelo couldn't have done any better.

While Jessen busied himself with ogling Ian's not-too-shabby appearance, if he did say so himself, Ian took advantage of their proximity to study this ghost from the past.

Jessen Sørensen's angelic face had haunted him. The feathered lashes, the full, pouty lips, the porcelain skin.

Fine, near-white hairs still brushed his hairline, but his locks were a rich gold now and curled in every direction. Soft waves that Ian itched to feel trailing down his back.

Oh no. Fuck, no.

He must have muttered the admonition aloud because Jessen's gaze snapped up to his, full of amusement. And lust.

The latter threatened to flatten Ian. He really needed to get the fuck out of there.

"Jesus…Christ," Jessen drawled, incredulous, his irises nearly black with want. "It's still there, isn't it?"

"Wh-what?" Ian wanted to crawl inside himself. Anything to protect him from the onslaught of Jessen's presence.

Too much too much too much.

"This."

Jessen closed the distance between them, bringing their chests flush. Thank *God* he didn't press his groin to Ian's, or he might have felt the effect their two-minute conversation.

He was weak, so weak when it came to Jessen Sørensen.

Ian had spent too many nights alone in bed, with his hand wrapped around his aching flesh, stroking it raw with images of this man in his head.

Jessen on his knees before him, Ian's cock in his mouth while he looked up, teary-eyed and blissed out just from pleasuring him. The memory of Jessen's mouth stretched around him was always enough to take him over the edge.

It had him there right now, and Ian shook his head in an attempt to dislodge the traitorous thoughts.

But his face was flush, and his breathing erratic, and Jessen knew him too. Knew his tells.

Fuck, fuck, fuck.

Jessen dipped his head, his breath ghosting over Ian's ear.

"I'm going to kiss you."

"No, you're not."

"Yes, I am."

"Why?"

It had come out as a whimper and Ian was fucking mortified. He was a grown man, why did this one person have such a hold on him? Seven years hadn't been enough to break it, and it made him angry. Livid.

"I don't want to kiss you," he protested as Jessen finally pressed their groins together.

Ian couldn't hold back his little, needy sigh as he felt the hard outline of Jessen's cock rub up against his own.

"Oh, young Ian…I think you do."

Fuck fuck fuck.

He did. He really did.

"No."

It was weak. Ian was so weak.

Jessen laughed under his breath, and it gave Ian a bit of strength.

How fucking dare he?

"I said no." Ian's voice was a little stronger this time, strong enough that it made Jessen pull back.

He searched Ian's face, and Ian tried to look resolute.

But he was shaking, and he could barely breathe. And a big part of him, a huge part of him, wanted nothing more than to say yes.

Yes, I want you. I've always wanted you.

Yes, I want this. I need it.

Please, don't stop.

But Jessen had heard his words, even if his body language had projected his internal debate. The taller man stepped back. Only a few inches, but it was enough.

Ian closed his eyes and counted backward from ten. In Latin. His grip on the countertop was so tight his knuckles hurt, and he concentrated on the pain. Let it ride him, let it push back his desire a little.

Exhaling, he finally opened his eyes and looked at Jessen.

Face flush, and pupils dilated, it was clear he wanted Ian, and that in itself was a small victory.

"I know you're not saying you don't want me to kiss you because you clearly do. In fact, I'd wager you want a whole lot more."

Ian was speechless. The nerve of this guy. The absolute, unmitigated gall.

"I sound arrogant, I know. But baby..."

"Don't," Ian spat before he could rein in his anger. "Don't."

Jessen gave him a slight nod. He licked his lower lip, drawing it into his mouth and Ian had to bite back another moan. That mouth of his was a fucking menace.

"I felt how much you want me, Ian."

There was nothing Ian could say to that, he was still hard as granite.

"So I am guessing the no has more to do with...how we parted ways."

A bitter laugh bubbled up from Ian's throat. "You're so fucking observant."

"Not always," Jessen said, sounding tired all of a sudden. "Listen, do you want to get out of here?"

"Yes. I do."

He smiled. "Yeah? Great, I live..."

"Not with you."

The smile fell away so quickly Ian almost felt regret.

"Ah."

"Please back up."

Jessen blinked, his mouth gaping like a fish out of water. "Oh. Right. Sorry."

He moved, and Ian finally took a full breath. His lungs burned. It was the effect of having Jessen Sørensen so close to him, Ian would always drown in the guy, and that was no good.

Easing past Jessen, careful not to touch him, Ian was grateful when the taller man let him escape without pursuit.

Or so he'd thought.

"You live around here, right?"

"What?" Ian turned back to him.

"You live nearby."

"Uh, yeah."

"Great, mind if I walk you home?"

Oh, shit. "That's probably not a good idea."

Jessen's playful, mischievous grin returned. "You worried I might wear you down?"

Ian rolled his eyes because, *yes*. "No, but…"

"*Fett*, I will walk you safely to your door." Jessen strolled past him and through to the hall, calling back. "Come on, then."

What in the holy hell was happening?

Ian followed. Apparently, that's what was happening.

Chapter 4

The walk was awkward, and not only on Ian's side. Jessen was uncharacteristically quiet. Ian had begun to wonder why he'd insisted on coming.

Gone was the overt flirtation. In its place, there was a nervous energy and Ian didn't know what to do with it.

The students were deep into their final exams, so the campus was quiet. It had rained during the party, and the ground was covered with leaves from the ancient trees that blanketed the UP campus.

"How do you like teaching?"

Those were not the first words Ian had expected from Jessen, but he was grateful for the normalcy.

"I love it," he confessed easily. "We get the brightest coming through here, and I love watching them fall in love with their theorems, develop new concepts, discover their own voices. It's very rewarding."

"You sound like an infomercial," Jessen countered, chuckling.

"Meaning?"

Smiling eyes flashed his way. "No offense, it's just that...you were always so passionate about film, and now you're helping people only a little younger than you develop their dreams. What about yours?"

My dream died the night you walked out on me.

"Film is just a hobby, this is what I was born to do. If I can impart a love for physics to this new generation…"

"It's the same generation, Ian. We're not much older than these grad students."

"Fine. Okay. Maybe I just feel like I'm not one of them."

"Because you set yourself apart from them long ago."

They turned off the quad and walked to the intersection to wait for the light. Ian thought about dismissing Jessen, telling him he'd had a long week and just wanted to get home to bed. It wasn't a lie, he was exhausted, but he knew sleep would evade him.

"You don't know me, Jess. Not anymore."

They crossed the street in silence. Beside him, Ian could practically hear Jessen formulating his response. But they were almost at his doorstep, there wouldn't be time to continue the conversation. Not without inviting him inside.

Which sure as fuck was not going to happen.

"That one's yours, isn't it?" Jessen pointed to the porch on Ian's Victorian townhouse.

He'd bought the place when it was in ruins and had spent two years restoring it himself. He loved the little house, which sat on Baring Street surrounded by nineteenth-century stone mansions and red brick, Federalist homes. Ian's house was an outlier, just like him.

"How do you know where I live?"

Jessen shrugged. "I've been in Philly for a few months, now."

"That explains nothing."

"I think it explains everything," Jessen countered, his voice a caress.

They stood at the bottom of Ian's steps. Three quick hops and a turn of a key, and he could be inside where it was safe. Away from the tempting enigma that stood beside him.

"Anyway…"

"Aren't you going to invite me in for a nightcap, or whatever?"

Ian arched his brows. "I wasn't, actually. No."

"Ouch." Jessen flattened his hand over his heart as if mortally wounded. "I'm surprised by how rude you've become, Ian."

Before he could react, Jessen slipped the keys out of Ian's hand and jogged up to the door. He chose the right key on his first try, because of course he did, and strolled into Ian's home like he belonged there.

Which he most certainly did not.

This was so fucked up, but Ian followed him inside and flicked on the lights.

Jessen whistled. "Fuck, Ian. This is beautiful!"

And it was. Ian had painted the walls of the main living space in Wedgewood blue, true to the period in which the house was built, and it set off the pristine, white wainscoting beautifully.

A large bay window let in plenty of light during the day and provided a comfortable reading spot at night. Oversized furniture in cream twill made up the bulk of the seating.

He'd transformed the formal dining room into a makeshift A-V suite, which housed his iMac and his Mac Pro, plus his other editing equipment. Unconventional, but it suited him.

"This is really nice, Ian," Jessen murmured, turning to him. "I'm really happy for you."

There was awe in his voice and reverence.

Ian suppressed the wave of pride that swept over him. Jessen was the only person he'd told about his tumultuous childhood, his deadbeat father, and disturbed mother. He was the only person he'd told about his dream of owning a beautiful home and planting roots in a community.

Most people never asked about the family of a prodigy, as long as the prodigy kept producing. Siv knew a bit about his wrecked childhood, but only Jessen knew it all. Every dark and dirty detail.

Ian had told Jessen everything one night, overwhelmed by the emotions spilling over him after their first time having sex. Making love. They'd done a lot before then, just about everything, but it wasn't until that night that they'd gone all the way.

Ian had given Jessen his all, every little bit of himself. Had spilled his heart and soul to the man who had cracked open his hard shell for the first time in his life.

And then he had woken up one morning to an empty space in the bed next to him, and a note on the floor.

I'm sorry.

He still had the note.

Those two words had splintered Ian into a million indiscernible pieces. Pieces he was still trying to fit back together.

And there stood Jessen Sørensen, in his fucking dining room, glowing like he kept his own personal sun somewhere behind his rib cage.

"Do you have any coffee?"

"Yes."

"Could I possibly get a cup?" A smile danced at the edges of his sinful mouth.

"No."

Jessen laughed. "Please?"

"There's a Char-bucks on the corner if you want coffee. I am not making you coffee, Jess."

"Aww," he pouted prettily. "Why not?"

Why not.

Why not.

"Why not?"

"Yeah." Jessen was grinning. No, he was *smirking*.

The bubbling volcano in Ian's belly erupted.

"Who the fuck do you think you are?"

The blond's eyes widened and the smirk melted away. "I…"

"Seven years, Jess. Seven. Fucking. Years. You walked out of my life in the middle of the goddamned night, no goodbye, nothing. Just 'I'm sorry' scratched on a piece of brown paper bag."

"I know, and I…"

"Shut the fuck up."

To his credit, Jessen did shut the fuck up.

To his credit, Ian wasn't screaming. Yet.

He turned on his heel and stalked into the living room, throwing himself onto the couch. It was big and plush and the first piece of furniture he'd purchased for the house.

His house.

His.

He felt like his safe haven had been invaded by the enemy from his heartbroken past.

Ian's chest heaved. There was so much he wanted to say, so much he'd bottled up and walled-off. And Jessen was right there. *Right there.*

The other man entered the room slowly, carefully. He sat on the coffee table across from Ian.

No one sat on the coffee table. It was an antique that had come with the house and Ian was proud of it. But he didn't give a shit right then. Fuck the goddamn coffee table and the man sitting on it in his five-hundred-dollar skinny jeans.

He wanted Jessen gone, and yet he was terrified to let him go.

"What do you want me to do?"

Ian blinked up at him, confused by this all-too-sober sounding Jessen. "What do you mean?"

"If you want me to leave, I will leave. Right now, just say the word. If you want me to give you some time, I will." His gaze softened. "If...if you want me to stay, I'll stay."

"What if I wanted you to leave Philly and never come back?" Ian eyed him carefully. "Would you do that?"

Jessen looked pained, but he nodded. "Eventually."

"What if I wanted you to go back in time and fix what you broke, could you?"

"God, I wish." He'd choked out the words.

Ian frowned. Studying Jessen, he noticed a slight hunch in his shoulders. There were dark circles under his eyes. He seemed smaller, dimmer. It was confusing, conflicting with the mental image he'd always carried.

"Why are you here?"

Jessen exhaled and rested his elbows on his knees. He knit his fingers together and faced Ian, his expression more serious than Ian had ever seen.

"I owe you an apology."

Ian snorted, he couldn't help it.

Jessen's smile was slight. "I know, seven years too late, but…I hope…I was hoping…"

"What? Thought you'd pop back up, bat those pretty eyes of yours, and I'd bend over for you?"

"You still think my eyes are pretty?"

"That's what you focus on?"

At least he had the grace to look contrite. "Sorry."

"Are you?"

Jessen's expression morphed into a mask of regret. "Yes, God. Yes. You have no idea how sorry I am. I ran away, Ian. I ran away from you, and I'll never forgive myself. Even if you somehow find a way to forgive me, I'll never forgive myself. I hurt you."

"You hurt me?"

"I know I did."

"No, Jess. You don't know shit. You didn't just hurt me, you broke me. You fucked up an already fucked-up kid." Ian ran a rough hand through his overgrown hair. "I could barely function after you disappeared. I missed classes, had to postpone my exams, I was a total wreck when you fucked off and out of my life."

Ian was shaking, his jaw trembling so hard his teeth chattered. And he was pissed because it shouldn't affect him this much anymore, not so many years after the fact. He was beyond this pain.

"Fuck, Ian…I'm so…" Jessen reached out as if he were going to touch him and Ian pressed himself back into the cushions.

He could not let that happen.

"I'm so sorry. God, that sounds lame. Even to me."

"Because it is lame. Sorry? Sorry was seven years ago. Six, maybe. I'd even give you five. But now?"

Jessen nodded. His gaze flicked toward the door, and Ian panicked.

The thought of letting him walk out in the middle of this long overdue conversation was almost paralyzing.

"Don't go."

Jessen's gaze snapped back to his. "What? No, I…"

"You were thinking of leaving."

He nodded. "Yes, but only to give you some space. I had no idea I'd cause...I didn't think you'd..."

"You thought I was over you."

Jessen's jaw hung open, his eyes wide. For the first time since he'd first met him, Ian saw fear in Jessen's eyes.

"Are you?"

Ian wanted to pretend. Wished he could. He wanted to lie, but even after so long he knew it was pointless. He was an open wound where Jessen Sørensen was concerned. He could never hide the bleeding from him.

"No, Jess. That's the problem. I'll never be over you."

Chapter 5

As soon as the words were out of his mouth, Ian wanted to swallow them back down. What a colossal fucking mistake, admitting a weakness like that to a guy like Jess.

He'd turned his gaze to the ceiling, unwilling to subject himself to the smug satisfaction that was sure to be in the other man's expression. So he wasn't prepared for the sob that echoed in the room.

Jessen's head was in his hands, those long fingers raking roughly through his hair while he whispered *fy faen* over and over. He was rocking, his leg bouncing wildly and shaking him all over.

"Jess?"

"Fuck."

"What is it?"

Concern had replaced every other emotion in Ian's body because this was Jessen Sørensen. The man, the myth, the living legend. Nothing rattled him, not then and not now.

He might not have ever admitted it aloud, but Ian had kept tabs on Jessen. His career, his exploits. The women. The men. There was always something in the tabloids about the Sørensen twins, rumors about their sexual conquests and epic parties.

Ian hadn't known what to believe, but none of it seemed outside the realm of possibility. Or probability.

But the man sitting across from him, clutching his hair and mumbling while he rocked to an unknown rhythm, this wasn't the man Ian knew.

"I am so fucked, Ian."

"What happened?"

Watery, blue eyes lifted to his and Ian's breath caught. Jesus. Fuck, he was so…fucking…beautiful. Even in his distress.

Jess sighed. He exhaled a long breath, and his body stilled. "God. That right there. That's what I need."

Confused, Ian frowned. "What?"

Before he could formulate another thought, Jessen had moved forward. The taller man had knelt between Jessen's thighs and had taken his face into his hands. He had only a second to process the abrupt change in the atmosphere when Jessen's mouth descended on his.

Heat flared in his belly, and Ian gasped into the kiss.

It was raw, feral, and a little bit frightening. Make that a lot frightening.

There was no finesse to Jessen's kiss. It was as if he were trying to wring something out of Ian. Something he desperately needed. But, oh, the taste of him.

Jessen's tongue swept into his mouth, his moans filled his ears, and Ian's body responded. Boy, did it respond. He ached.

After having gone so long without him, Ian felt like he'd stumbled upon a fresh, mountain spring while wandering in the desert.

His heart soared, despite his efforts to clip its wings. Because this wasn't paradise, it was a mirage. Whatever was going on with Jessen, it had nothing to do with him.

Breaking away, Ian tried to catch his breath.

Jessen pushed him back, eased him down onto his back while he attacked his neck with lips, teeth, and tongue before reclaiming his mouth. The kisses were heady, needy.

Ian heard him mumble under his breath and caught a few words in his native Norwegian.

Fy faen, jeg har savnet deg.
Trenger deg, ikke send meg bort.

"Wait." Ian pushed back, cupping his hands over Jessen's shoulders. "Jess, wait."

Jessen dropped his head to Ian's chest, his own heaving, but allowed him to sit up.

Ian didn't know what to do with his hands, so he cupped them around Jessen's neck.

The other man sighed like the weight of the universe was on his shoulders. He knelt between Ian's thighs and clung to him like a lifeline.

"You wanna tell me what the hell is going on?" Ian could barely catch his breath, but he needed answers.

Jessen nodded into his clavicle. "Give me a minute."

"Yeah. Sure."

The memories were brutal. A warm spring night just like that one when a nineteen-year-old Ian had finally embraced who he was and what he wanted. Who he wanted. All thanks to the man currently curled up in his arms.

Jessen had been his first and very nearly his only. Would have been, were it not for Siv and her insistence that he not let his past dictate his future.

Plenty of fish in the sea, she'd said. And there were.

Ian had enjoyed the company of quite a few over the years, but no one had ever come close to owning him. There was only one white whale.

"I should start at the beginning." Jessen's grip tightened where he'd buried his fingers into Ian's Henley. "You deserve to know everything."

"Okay."

Blue eyes, rimmed in red but still so blue. The prettiest blue Ian had ever seen. They blinked up at him when Jessen raised his head. He pulled back, settling next to Ian on the couch. Still, he grabbed Ian's hands as if he were afraid he might run away.

"I'm here," Ian said without thinking.

Jessen's expression darkened. "Jesus, Ian. What the fuck did I do to you?"

Slowly, he reached out and cupped Ian's cheek. It was so gentle a touch that a lump formed in Ian's throat. It was all he'd ever wanted, seven years ago. This was surreal.

"I know," Jessen said, a smile threatening to curve one side of his mouth. "This feels like a dream. I can't believe I'm here."

"*You* can't believe it?"

Jessen ducked his eyes, dropping his hand to Ian's lap where he held onto his other hand.

"You must have hated me this entire time."

"Yes." There was no point in denying it.

Jessen nodded. "Rightly so, I..." He swallowed.

"From the beginning."

His blue gaze flicked up and back down. "Okay, from the beginning."

Jessen squeezed Ian's hands, and Ian squeezed back.

"First, let me say something." He looked up from under his golden lashes. "I never stopped thinking about you."

Ian snorted. "I never knew you thought of me at all. I was convinced you didn't care. Still am, to be honest."

Jessen frowned. "How could you doubt it?"

"You can't be serious. How could I doubt it? You left, Jess."

"Yeah, but...I left because was so into you I couldn't keep my head on straight."

Ian yanked his hands away. "Wait. What? That...that makes zero sense. And it's bullshit, I'm calling bullshit."

Jessen reached for him, entwining their fingers. "It's not. I ran away because I was fucking terrified. I was a kid."

"You were twenty-two."

"Still a kid."

"I was the kid, Jess. I was an innocent before I met you. A battered and bruised one. A reject until I met you, and you made me feel like I was worth something."

"You were, you are," Jessen hastened to say.

"You made me feel like I was someone that somebody could… could love."

"Fuck, Ian, you are." Jessen ran a hand through Ian's hair that unspooled a thread of pleasure down his spine.

"Then why are you sitting here telling me you left because you were too *into me*?"

"I left because I thought I was going to ruin you."

"So you left to *save* me? Is that it? More bullshit."

"It's not bullshit!" Jessen's voice echoed off the plaster walls, and Ian winced. "Sorry. Sorry, I just…I need you to hear me."

"Talk, then. From the beginning, you said."

"When Mattias got his record deal, remember we were in a band together. Sol Brothers?"

"I still think it was a cheesy name," Ian interjected.

Jessen smiled. "It was, but we were pretty good. Right? Very good, actually. We went on to play a bunch of festivals. That's how we caught the attention of the label in Florida. They put is on tour with Yara, that pop singer."

"Doesn't exactly sound like a horror story."

"It wasn't, not at first. But when the deal came, it wasn't for Sol Brothers, it was for Mattias. Marcus Kaine, that's the head of the label, he only wanted Mattias as a solo act."

"Matty S."

Jessen nodded. "Yeah. I was still quote-unquote *a part of things*, but he was the name. The face."

Ian frowned. "You're twins."

The other man laughed, and it was entirely devoid of mirth.

"We're similar, but not the same. Matt, he has that…that thing that draws people to him. I can't explain it. He's always been that way. It's like people can't resist him. He could ask them to walk off of a roof, and they'd line up to do it."

"Uh, Jess, you have it too, whatever it is."

His smile was sardonic. "No, I don't. And I wouldn't want to."

"Are you dense? Even at Siv's party, people were hovering around you. And they hadn't ever met you before."

"Nah, that's just the after-effect of being Matt's brother. I look enough like him that people know who I am and want to know the behind-the-scenes gossip. They want the inside scoop on all my brother's exploits."

"And yours."

Jessen shrugged. "And mine, I guess."

"Don't be facetious, Jessen. You aren't exactly a hanger-on in Matty's life. You're a full participant."

Both blond eyebrows arched. "And you know this based on...?"

Busted. Ian took a breath.

"I...look, you're practically a household name. And since you disappeared on me, I sure as fuck wasn't going to try and call you. I had to resort to stalking you via the tabloids. And your Instagram. Well, Matty's, since you don't have one. I'm well aware of your...lifestyle."

Jessen smiled. It was crazy sexy, and Ian looked away.

He leaned in close, his breath tickling Ian's hair. "I'm going to ignore the dig and focus on the fact that you stalked me by reading tabloid news. You, the intellectual."

Ian scoffed. "Me, the intellectual, was in love with you."

Jessen's breath hitched, and Ian squeezed his eyes shut.

What the fuck had made him say that? Proximity. It was having Jessen so close, and so beautiful still, it...it was too much.

The blond was on him in a flash.

Warm hands cupped his face. Warm, soft lips closed around his own. The neediest of sighs fanned out over his cheek as Jessen kissed him. Insistent hands gripped his biceps, pulling him forward against a hard chest.

Suddenly, the seven years were erased. It was as it had been before. Like time hadn't passed.

Jessen was hungry, and Ian was eager to be devoured, hands fisting into the soft weave of Jessen's t-shirt. But no.

No.

Pushing him away, Ian got to his feet and paced the room.

"I can't do this. N-not again."

He gripped his own hips. Hard. Ian didn't trust himself not to reach out to the other man. Not to allow himself to be pulled him back into his arms.

It was a craving.

It was a curse.

Breathless and shaken, Jessen stood mere feet away. "Maybe I should go."

"Maybe you should." Ian nodded frantically, still unable to catch his breath.

He couldn't look at him, too afraid he'd beg Jessen to stay. Or throw himself at him like the lovesick teenager he'd been when they'd first met.

Jessen had the sense not to come near him as he walked to the front door, but he moved slowly. As if he were hoping Ian would stop him.

Ian had no intention.

The sound of the door clicking open reverberated off the walls of Ian's home. It had never seemed so loud. So damning.

"For the record," Jessen said as he slipped back into the night. "I'm not staying away this time."

Chapter 6

Seven Years Ago

Ian had always loved school. It had always been a kind of refuge for him, the only setting that had ever made sense. You studied, you were tested, you passed, or you failed. Very little room for ambiguity, even in a field as subjective as theoretical physics.

If he kept his head down, did the work, put in the time, did his best, good things would come. It was a lesson he'd learned at an early age.

But it was never a tactic that had worked for him at home.

With an absentee father, a mentally unstable mother, and having bounced from relative to relative until no one could be bothered anymore, Ian had landed on his feet.

More or less.

Making his way across the cold, wet University of Philadelphia campus, he was having second thoughts.

He loved the faculty at UP, no question. But his classmates, his peers… Well, the problem was that Ian had no peers.

At nineteen, he was the youngest Ph.D. candidate the school had ever admitted. There had never been a question. He'd begun his post-secondary career at UP, and he would stay there for the rest of his life if he could. Safe in the bubble the school had created for him.

Students came and went, UP remained the same. The only constant Ian had ever known.

Pushing through the glass doors of Holm Hall, Ian shook off the rain droplets that had gathered on the surface of his hoodie.

"There he is." Siv Bergdahl, a Mathematical Physics post-grad and Ian's assigned mentor, pulled him into a hug as soon as he was somewhat dry.

Though he complained about her excessive compulsion to show him affection, he secretly loved it. Siv was the only person he'd ever felt comfortable enough to hug for any length of time, and she indulged herself frequently.

"I promised I'd be here, and I never break a promise."

She smiled. "I know little one. It's one of the many things I adore about you."

"So, I'm here. Explain to me what I'm supposed to do?"

"Did you bring your camera?"

"Yeah." Ian shook the water off his backpack before unzipping it and retrieving his camera case. "You need me to film your lecture?"

"Oh, no." Siv laughed. "I'm lending you out to campus activities tonight."

Ian froze. "You...what? Why?"

"Don't panic. You won't have to do anything stressful like talk to people your own age." She poked him playfully. "Well, maybe a little."

Ian scowled, but her lovely green eyes only blinked up innocently. "What do they need me to do?"

"There's a band playing at the Hub tonight, and apparently they're really, really popular on college radio. C.A. wants to document having them here, for when they get big, I guess."

Despite his protestations, Ian could already picture the end result. He loved watching old concert footage, marveling at how film could transport the viewer to the live event itself.

"I can see your wheels turning, poppet." Siv grinned and pinched his cheek, earning her an eye roll.

"Fine, whatever. What time does it start?"

Siv checked her watch. "In an hour, so get over there if you want some behind-the-scenes stuff."

Ian zipped up his slightly damp hoodie and hoisted his backpack back onto his shoulder after making sure the camera gear was safely tucked inside.

"I'm only doing this for you. I have a paper due in two days on neutrinos."

"You'll thank me," she said as he pushed through the doors and back into the rain. "Besides, you need balance in your life, dear. Balance!'

The first thing Ian heard when he finally entered the Hub was the monotonous *pop pop pop pop* of a snare drum as it cracked the air and Ian's eardrums.

"That's fine, move on to the kick," came a voice over the P.A. system.

Thump thump thump thump thump. The drummer idly tapped the pedal while the sound engineer checked the levels on his board.

Ian had gotten there too early. The band wasn't even into their sound check yet.

Ah, well.

He gave his eyes time to adjust to the darkness of the hall before he wound his way toward the dressing room.

"Are you supposed to be here?" A silver-haired man in his late forties/early fifties addressed Ian as if he'd trespassed on his lawn.

Ian held up his camera bag. "I'm with the student staff. Here to film."

"Ah, right." The man nodded. "Go on back, they're probably doing vocal warm ups."

Ian could hear faint voices through the thick velvet curtains that separated the backstage area from the front room. He followed the sound until he found a door that had been left slightly ajar. Through it, he could make out a short, olive-skinned guy with a head full of dark curls.

Ian pushed the door open, ready to introduce himself when the room burst into laughter.

The dark-haired guy doubled over with mirth and Ian felt himself smile. He was cute, the guy, and his laugh was infectious. Pushing the door wide open, Ian stepped inside the room and stopped. Everything stopped.

His brain, his breath, his heart.

Two tall, lanky blonds clasped each other as they laughed to the point of tears. For a moment, Ian thought he was seeing double but, no. There were two of them.

Beautiful.

They were beautiful. Twins, he thought, though his gaze kept drifting to the one on the left. His smile was pure sunshine. Long-limbed but not slight, with blond hair that jutted out the top of his head in unruly waves, and lake-blue eyes, Ian couldn't stop staring at him. That is until the other man noticed.

The guy's laugh had faltered for only a second before a rosy, pink tongue crept forward to tease the tip of one of his fang-like canines. His expression was downright lascivious, and Ian blushed.

It only made the other man's smile grow even brighter. His blue eyes twinkled as Ian struggled to find words, and the room took notice of him.

"You alright, bud?" The dark-haired guy frowned and then laughed, his gaze bouncing back and forth between Ian's and the twin on the left. "That's Mattias and Jessen, I'm Jacob."

Ian's mouth, which had been hanging open, snapped shut. He swallowed.

"Hey, I, uh...Ian. I'm Ian."

"You here to shoot us? That's chill."

Ian nodded and busied himself with extracting the camera from his bag, grateful to have something to do with his hands because they trembled. He could feel Jessen's eyes on him and his neck heated.

It was annoying.

"Make sure you get my good side," yelled a softly accented, male voice. Ian didn't dare look up.

"All of your sides are good, Matty."

Ian recognized Jacob's voice and chanced a look behind him. The brothers' arms were draped around each other's shoulders. To the naked eye, they seemed intoxicated, but Ian noted the bottles of water in their hands.

They drank in sync. Laughed in sync at something else Jacob had said, something Ian had missed because he'd been staring again. And, again, he got caught.

Jessen. The beautiful brother – okay, really they were both gorgeous, but this one...*the* one sauntered over to where Ian crouched down over his backpack.

"Do you need help?"

Ian kept his eyes on the guy's feet while he pulled out his tripod. "No, thanks."

"You sure?"

Long legs bent at the knees, and suddenly Ian was eye-to-eye with heaven.

Oh, God, he thought. *Oh, hell.*

The desire was a punch to the groin, and Ian sucked in a quick breath.

"Jessen," the other man breathed, a smile tugging at the corner of his mouth. "In case you were wondering which of us was which."

"I wasn't." Ian dropped his gaze back to his equipment, needlessly fidgeting with the light meter.

"No?" There was so much humor and warmth in the one syllable that Ian looked up and was immediately lost in a blue labyrinth.

He slowly shook his head while his mouth seemed to go on autopilot.

"I can tell you apart."

The blond's eyebrows flicked up, and he smiled, then shrugged. "Yeah? Well, it's because he's the pretty one."

"No." Ian's heart thumped hard in his chest. "No, he isn't."

Whatever words Jessen had been about to say died on his tongue. Ian watched it happen, watched his lips move and fail to produce any sound.

They locked gazes and the world around them fell away. All Ian heard, saw, smelled was Jessen. It scared him half to death. He took a shaky breath, his eyelids fluttering maddeningly.

Jessen's smile brightened, and his gaze flicked down to Ian's mouth.

Christ.

"How old are you, Ian?"

"I'll be twenty soon," he answered without thinking.

That bright smile morphed into something else, something deadly.

"*Det er godt å vite,*" he all but whispered, staring at Ian's lips like he wanted to launch himself at them. "Very good to know."

Ian's heart hammered so loud in his chest he was sure the whole concert hall could hear it. And yet, he could not look away from those eyes. That face. That fucking mouth. He was drunk off the vision of this man.

"Jess!"

The spell broken, Ian inhaled sharply. Somewhere along the way, he'd stopped breathing, and now he was lightheaded.

"Yeah?" Jessen answered but kept his eyes on Ian.

"Get your ass on stage," Mattias called after him. "We're late for the sound check. And stop flirting with the staff."

The broad smile returned as Jessen stretched to his full height. His gaze never left Ian's. "Now, where would be the fun in that?"

Chapter 7

Present Day

Ian dragged himself out of bed an hour before his alarm sounded. The night had been rough, one of the roughest he'd had in a long time.

He hadn't been able to sleep, hadn't been able to concentrate on his students' projects. He'd been fucking useless and all because of Jessen.

Fuck, the guy was poison. Pretty poison.

Ian's shower was cursory, and he didn't even bother with breakfast, just walked the few blocks to his office on campus and sank into his weathered old chair.

The place smelled of old books and new ideas. Ian loved it. Other than his house, and maybe Siv's place, his office was the only space that felt like home to Ian.

"Knock, knock." Martin Fassen stuck his head in the door. "How goes?"

"It goes."

"Hmm." He entered the room and took the chair opposite. "Someone needs coffee."

Ian nodded. "Only if it can be administered intravenously. I barely made it out of bed this morning."

"Rough night with your papers?"

Martin had sat next to him in Ian's film class when he was an undergrad, and the two had struck up a friendship. Now, Fassen was an adjunct professor. They sometimes went for a beer after work.

He knew better than to assume Ian had done anything else on a late night than grade papers or work on his film hobby.

He'd also been there for Ian's dark, post-Jessen days, though he never learned the cause of Ian's meltdown.

"Something like that."

Ian fired up his PC and scrolled through his email. There were dozens of frantic pleas from his second-year students hoping to raise their borderline grades with extra credit. Ian turned off his monitor.

"I can't do this today."

"Ian, what's going on?" The concern in Martin's voice made Ian turn to him.

"I'm okay."

"Define 'okay.' Buddy, I've known you for a while now. I haven't seen you look this lost since, well…"

Since the last time Jessen was in town, though Martin didn't know the details.

"I…" Ian started, not knowing what to say.

How did one explain carrying a seven-year torch for someone who wasn't worth the match it took to light one?

"Is it a girl?"

"No." Ian offered a half-grin. "Not a girl."

"A guy?"

Ian's gaze shot to Martin's.

"Don't look so panicked," Martin said, chuckling. "I think I've known for a while. Probably since we were back in class together, that semester you sort of checked out of everything."

Ian stared at him in shock.

"Are you waiting for me to judge you or something? Dude, it's the twenty-first century."

"Right." Ian nodded. "Sorry."

Martin waved him off. "Are you okay, though? Really?"

"No," Ian replied, his mouth on auto-pilot.

"Anything you need to unload?"

Martin sat back in his chair, crossing his ankle over his knee as if settling in for the long haul.

Ian took a moment to study the man. His open, inviting demeanor put one at ease.

Martin was good people.

Ian wondered why he hadn't cultivated more of a friendship with him. Well, he knew why. He didn't do the people thing very well.

Still, Martin sat there waiting. Listening.

And Ian opened his mouth. "Do you remember when I…seven years ago when I…"

"When you imploded?"

Ian snorted, the tension easing out of his shoulders. "Yeah."

Martin nodded and scratched the back of his neck before pulling at the collar of his navy blue Polo shirt.

"I'm going to ask you a question before you continue if that's okay."

"Sure."

"Was it that guy? The musician?"

Fuck, had he been so transparent?

Ian nodded.

"Thought so, go on." Martin knit his fingers on his knee and smiled.

"Jessen, that's his name."

"Wait." Martin's eyes widened. He sat forward on the chair and lowered his voice. "Jessen Sørensen? The former rock god-turned-guitar instructor who just joined the music department?"

Ian's pulse tripped over itself. "The what of the *what?*"

"He came on a month ago, took over Bobby Eckard's spot. I finally met him at Siv's little party last night."

Ian gaped at him. "He…he's teaching here now?"

"Across campus, but yes." Martin cocked his head. "That's the guy who messed you up?"

"Fuck."

Martin whistled low. "Dude, that's…"

He shook his head.

"It's fucked up. But, hey, he's across campus. Chances are, you'll never run into him." He studied Ian for a breath. "Unless you want to run into him. Wait, did you run into him last night?"

Ian nodded again, still at a loss for words.

"Oh, shit!" Martin laughed and then coughed to cover it. "Sorry, but this is some teen drama shit. Did you guys, you know…?"

"Fuck, Martin. No, we didn't *you know*. Not last night and not ever again." Ian ran a hand through his hair. He'd forgotten to comb it, not that it mattered. "I had no idea he was back in Philly. Siv didn't know he was, you know, *the guy*. She introduced us."

"And now you look like you've been run over by a herd of boy bands."

Ian rustled up a scowl. "Don't be an ass."

"Sorry," Martin said while sounding not very sorry at all. "I have years of jokes stored up for you. For instance-"

"Stop right there."

Martin winked. "I'm kidding. I'm not that guy, Ian. But I am a little put out you felt you had to keep me in the dark."

"About me being gay?"

"Are you? Gay?"

"Yeah, why?"

Martin shrugged one shoulder. "Just want to know the proper term. You could be bisexual or pansexual, or…"

Ian shook his head. "Nope, plain ol' boring gay."

"Cool, cool." Martin nodded. "So back to the Ex."

"We weren't together long enough for him to be considered an Ex." Ian frowned. "I don't think."

Martin narrowed his eyes. "Buddy… You were a fucking wreck after he left town the last time. Seriously, I thought you were terminally ill."

"No, just terminally stupid."

The other man's expression turned sympathetic. "You were twenty, and you had it bad. Was he your first?"

"I don't think we're at that stage of our friendship, Marty."

"If you're comfortable enough to finally call me Marty, then you can confide in me about anything." He leaned forward and put his hand on the desk between them. "Really, Ian. I'm a good listener."

Ian smiled. "I know, and thanks."

Martin sat back. "So what's your plan?"

"Avoid Jessen Sørensen until I retire or he does, whichever comes first."

"Shitty plan."

"What would you do?"

Martin seemed to put serious thought into the question.

Ian watched his wheels turn, feeling a little better than he had when he'd walked into the office.

"Well, no offense, but it's obvious he still has some hold over you."

Ian opened his mouth to contradict but snapped it shut just as quickly. "So?"

"So you have two choices: you can confront him, fuck him, and get him out of your system."

"Jesus, Marty."

"*Or*," he continued. "You can pretend he's in Siberia and you're allergic to the cold."

⸻

NEITHER OPTION PROVED VIABLE.

Over the next few days, Ian saw Jessen everywhere. In the cantina, in the bookstore, at the coffee shop.

It got to the point where Ian thought Jessen was indeed stalking him. Only, most of the time, he had been there when Ian arrived.

Still, he managed not to have any direct contact with the guy which made things marginally bearable. Only marginally because Ian had zero control over his dreams.

At night, Jessen Sørensen would wreak merry havoc on Ian's

subconscious, simultaneously laughing at him while also leaving him a shivering, quivering wet mess. He'd come dangerously close to coming in his sleep twice in the last week alone.

It just wouldn't do, but there wasn't much Ian could do about it. Jessen was giving him the space he'd demanded, and it was driving him insane.

So when he walked into his office one afternoon and found a note in Jessen's beautiful, sprawling script laying on his desk, he nearly wept with relief.

> *Ian,*
>
> *I know we aren't friends, but I have a new piece I really need you to hear. I'll be practicing this afternoon from two to four. Andem Hall, room 202. Please come.*
>
> *Klem,*
>
> *J*

Jessen's music was a definite weakness for Ian, and the thought of being alone in a room with him while he played was terrifying, but Ian wasn't sure he could resist.

He'd asked Ian to come and listen, wanted his opinion after all this time. All the distance. All the pain. It spoke volumes.

When two-thirty rolled around, Ian found himself standing on the second floor of Andem Hall. He heard a familiar chord progression, something from one of Jess and Matt's band days, and it catapulted Ian back in time.

Chapter 8

Seven years ago

Ian managed to get the video camera set up and scoped out the best locations to shoot stills of the band during their show. He also managed to avoid Jessen, an easier task while the band ran through their sound check.

Unfortunately for Ian, Jessen made a beeline for him as soon as they finished. And as luck would have it, Ian was in the darkest corner of the room with very few escape routes.

"Hello again."

"Hi." Ian made a show of leveling the tripod. He could feel Jessen's interest in him pouring over his skin in concussive waves. He rocked on his heels with each one, his breaths coming short and fast. Unable to stand it anymore, he turned to look at the blond.

Big. Mistake.

The hunger in Jessen's eyes made Ian woozy. He'd never been on the receiving end of that much focused intent.

"What do you want?" He asked trying to sound more annoyed than aroused.

"You," Jessen responded, shrugging one shoulder. "What are you doing after the show?"

"I…I'm going back to my dorm."

Jessen grinned. "Let me rephrase. *Who* are you doing after the show?"

"What?"

"Do you have a girlfriend?"

"N-no."

"Boyfriend?"

"No! Why…why would you ask that?"

"Oh," Jessen's gaze softened and so did his voice. "You're a baby gay."

He inched closer to Ian, gnawing on his plump bottom lip.

"Does anyone know?"

"Know what? What's to know?" Ian was practically hyperventilating.

"Shhh." Jessen reached out and placed a gentle hand on Ian's cheek. The effect was immediate and transformative.

Ian leaned into the touch like it was the source of the oxygen in his bloodstream. He actually swayed on his feet.

"*Faen*, you're sweet." Jessen's words ghosted over Ian's forehead as the blond moved closer, towering over him. The affection and warmth on his face were unexpected.

For one terrifying moment, Ian thought the guy was going to kiss him. Jessen's thumb swept over his cheek, then across his bottom lip.

"Wh-what are you doing?"

Jessen shook his head slightly, one errant curl swaying over his perfectly arched brows.

"I have no idea."

Looking up, Ian was shocked to see the uncertainty in Jessen's expression. He'd been cock-sure, so devastatingly direct, and this new revelation helped Ian to regain his sense of self.

He straightened and met his gaze.

Jessen searched his eyes and then dropped his hand to his side.

Ian felt the loss acutely.

"Will you wait for me after the show?"

"Why?"

"I just want to talk."

"You want to do more than talk."

Jessen grinned, but it was so different from before. Ian grinned back.

"I do, you're right, but…I do want to talk. First."

"And if all I want to do is talk?"

Jessen's sunshine smile returned. "Then talk is all we'll do, young Ian."

"Young? You can't be much older."

"I'm twenty-two."

"Oh." Ian bit his lip and swore he heard Jessen groan.

The blond stepped forward, and Ian froze. They were inches apart. Ian could smell the soap and sweat on Jessen's skin when he reached up to brush the hair out of his eyes.

"What am I going to do with you, baby gay?"

Ian exhaled a shaky breath. "Talk. We're going to talk."

Jessen searched his gaze, his smile dissolving into heat.

"And if I want to do more than talk?"

Ian tried to hide the shiver that shook his limbs.

"We talk. First."

THE SHOW WAS FANTASTIC.

Siv had said the guys were popular, and he could see why. The musicianship was tight. The Sørensen twins were beautifully trained but also had the something extra that all great artists seem to have.

Jacob was a beast on the bass guitar, and all three of them harmonized like a dream. Mattias was born to stand front and center. He had the crowd eating out of the palms of his hands.

Ian was impressed. But it wasn't until Mattias relinquished the microphone and allowed Jessen to step in as lead vocalist that Ian lost all sense of place and time.

The spotlight seemed to be absorbed into the gold of Jessen's hair and the pale skin of his face and hands as he cupped the microphone close to his mouth. His guitar, a thin, sleek, blade of an instrument hung low on his hips, all but forgotten as he closed his eyes swayed to the song's intro.

Then out poured the rawest, the most haunting tenor Ian had ever heard.

> *I was running in circles but afraid of coming 'round.*
> *I knew that I was lost and needed to be found.*

Jessen's ache, his need, it was all there in every note.

Ian was transfixed. Riveted to the spot, the camera in his hand heavy. Without thinking, he lifted it and peered through the lens.

Snap

He'd silenced the shutter, so only a whisper disturbed the space between Jessen's words.

A sea of people, nearly two hundred, filled the space between where Ian stood and where Jessen sang, but when he lifted his eyes to the crowd, Ian felt them land on him.

He dropped the camera to his side, unable to do more than stare.

> *I was looking for direction. Instead, you gave me your light.*
> *And though it was amazing, I knew it wasn't right.*
> *It wasn't quite right.*

Jessen looked haunted. Pained. Hungry.

And Ian couldn't look away.

Not when the song ended. Not when the show was done. He watched every little move Jessen made, all of the quick glances to make sure Ian was still there waiting. He was. He had no choice.

By the time Jessen handed off his guitar to a roadie and made his way through the thicket of admirers seeking autographs and photos, Ian was desperate. For what, he didn't know, just…desperate.

"Can we get out of here?"

Ian nodded. Together they packed up his equipment in silence.

"Jess, you hanging out? These ladies say there's a party." Mattias clasped a hand on Jessen's shoulder, two gorgeous girls on either side.

One had olive skin and dark blond hair with lighter highlights that streaked through the tresses like lightning strikes. Her hazel eyes were already half-lidded, either from booze or lust.

The other was equally as lovely, with a cinnamon complexion and dark, dark eyes. She was curvier than the other girl, her figure like an hour glass.

Jessen's gaze swept over the girls, one of his eyebrows quirking. He liked what he saw, that much was clear. But then he turned back.

"I have plans," he said over his shoulder, his eyes in Ian's.

Mattias looked at Ian then and grinned. "Of course you do."

Ian bet Jessen had "plans" after every show in every city. What had he been thinking? He turned away and zipped up his hoodie. The feel of Jessen's hand on his waist made him jump.

"Relax, we'll talk. Right?" That deep, smoky voice was right in his ear, and Ian had never been so instantly hot for another human being.

He nodded quickly and pulled away before he did something stupid like kiss him.

They were walking toward the door when the weight of the bag on Ian's shoulder eased.

"Let me," Jessen said, taking it onto his own shoulder.

"Uh, thanks."

With nothing to do with his hands, Ian shoved them into his pockets.

"So, did you like the show?"

Ian nodded. "Yeah."

"That's it? Just 'yeah'?" He expressed mock-offense, holding his hand to his chest.

"It was good."

Jessen nudged his shoulder. "Not a music fan?"

"I am. I'm a big music fan."

"Oh yeah?" The blond's eyebrow arched. "What do you listen to?"

"Nothing you've heard of. Obscure, nineties hip-hop, mostly."

Jessen laughed. "Really? You? That's not what I would have guessed."

"What would you have guessed?"

The blond shrugged. "Maybe Radiohead or Bon Iver. Something appropriately pretentious."

Ian stopped. "Radiohead is *not* pretentious."

The guy just grinned, one little dimple showing on his left cheek. "Gotcha."

Chapter 9

It was a Saturday night and the campus was hopping with parties and gatherings in nearly every corner.

As they walked, they were forced apart by gangs of drunken youths stumbling to their next watering hole. Quite a few heads turned Jessen's way as they passed.

"Did you have plans tonight?"

They'd fallen back into step, and Ian realized a little too late that they were nearly to his dorm.

"No, I was just going to study."

Jessen chuckled. "On a Saturday night?"

"I have a paper due on Monday."

"Yeah? On what?"

"High-powered proton beams and liquid metal targets."

Jessen whistled. "That sounds very…"

"Boring?"

He chuckled. "No, not boring. I was going to say intense. And advanced for an undergrad."

"I'm post-grad."

Jessen stopped. "You're nineteen."

Ian turned to face him, shrugging. "Prodigy."

"Seriously?" The blond's eyebrows shot up. "Wow, a real live genius."

Ian ducked his head.

"I wouldn't say that."

"I bet your friends would."

The pavement was uneven where they stood, and Ian kicked at a pebble that had broken off the concrete slab. It bounced along the hard surface until it finally disappeared in the grass.

"I wouldn't know."

Ian started walked again, and Jessen walked alongside him.

"No friends?"

"Not many. One or two."

"And why is that?"

It had stopped raining, but the air was still pregnant with moisture, waiting to give birth.

A familiar sense of unease settled in Ian's gut at Jessen's question. It was one he'd heard a lot.

"Not good with people, I guess."

They were in front of his dorm, and Ian took the bag from Jessen's shoulder.

"This is me."

Jessen looked up at the stately building. The gray masonry had been nearly completely overgrown by rich, green ivy.

"This campus is beautiful. Reminds me a little of home."

"Where's that?"

Jessen's blue eyes met his. They were dark in the dim light from the streetlamps.

"Oslo, though Mattias and I live in New York, now." He squinted and ran a hand through his hair. "Well, I say *live*, we're not there much. Life on the road, and all."

"That must get old."

He nodded. "It does."

"Anyway…" Ian started to turn.

"Aren't you going to invite me in?"

Ian stared at him. "You…you still want to?"

Jessen smiled. "Of course! Why wouldn't I?"

"I-I thought…"

The blond stepped up to him. "You thought *I'm a nerdy almost-twenty-year-old and no rock star is going to want to spend time with me.* Am I right?"

Ian rolled his eyes but couldn't fight the grin. "You're not a rock star."

"Not yet," Jessen winked as he ran his tongue over his front teeth. "You may be a little nerdy, young Ian, but there's one thing you don't seem to realize."

"Yeah? What?"

"You're fucking *hot.* And that you're brilliant too only makes you that much hotter."

Ian nearly choked on his tongue. "I-I'm not…"

Before he could process this bit of information, he felt Jessen's lips – those full, soft, pink-as-taffy lips – on his.

The kiss was quick but devastating, and Ian was left in a daze. He didn't even have time to worry about being seen in public kissing another guy.

"Come on then, young Ian." Jessen strolled past him and up the steps. "Show me your lair."

***

"So, you graduated high school when you were thirteen?"

Ian nodded. "Yeah. I would have done it sooner, but I took a month off to study abroad."

Jessen's eyes widened with something like awe. "*Serr?*"

"Hmm?"

He shook his head, chuckling. "Sorry, the Norwegian slips out. You seriously studied abroad when you were thirteen?"

"Twelve. It was a MENSA program." Ian nodded. "I was only gone for a month, but…it was probably the best month of my life."

"Wow, I bet."

"I…I didn't have the best childhood, so going away really opened my mind to my possibilities."

Jessen frowned. "I'm sorry to hear that but happy you found your calling."

"My calling?"

He nodded. "Just hearing you talk about science, the way your eyes light up, it's clear that it's your calling."

"I don't know," Ian replied, thinking. "I love film too."

"Really?"

"You sound surprised."

"A little. It's not very…practical."

Ian laughed, more tension fading from his body. "I'm not a very practical guy."

Jessen looked around Ian's room. The décor was spartan, except for a few movie posters on one wall. *Amelie*, *Yojimbo*, and *What Dreams May Come*.

"I see that," the blond said, smirking.

They sat on the floor of Ian's room, their backs against the bed, and it was nice. Easy.

Ian found it effortless to hold a conversation with the guy, although his brain frequently short-circuited when Jessen smiled.

It was radiant, life-affirming, and made Ian want things he shouldn't. But he'd had a taste of those lips and couldn't help but want more.

"Ian?"

"Hmm?"

"You're staring." Jessen grinned and cocked his head.

"Shit. Sorry." Ian shoved his hands into his hoodie and ducked his head.

"Hey."

A finger under his chin made him lift his face to Jessen's. They were a breath apart, and Jessen's gaze darted down to Ian's mouth and back.

"Young Ian?"

"Hmm?"

"I know I didn't ask permission to kiss you before, and that was wrong of me. I'm sorry."

"It's okay," Ian managed to croak. "S'fine."

"Yeah?" Those eyebrows flicked up again. "Would it be okay if I did it again?"

Ian thought he nodded, he couldn't be sure because his vision blurred the moment Jessen's intent became apparent.

The first kiss was tentative, and Ian thought he had heard Jessen's breath stutter before he tilted his head for a better angle. His lips were warm and soft, so soft.

Ian had kept his eyes open, unable to wrap his head around the fact that this was actually happening. But they fluttered closed when Jessen's hand cupped his cheek.

They broke apart, and Ian finally remembered to take a breath.

He opened his eyes to find Jessen gazing down at him, a dreamy expression on his beautiful face. He hadn't known anyone could ever look at him like that. Like they needed to kiss him, or bad things might happen.

"*Faen*," Jessen swore under his breath a second before reclaiming Ian's mouth.

Ian had kissed a few girls, though only one guy, none of whom had left him shaking and panting like Jessen had.

The second kiss was decidedly different from the first, designed to draw Ian outside his own body.

Both of Jessen's hands were on his face. And when his tongue swept across Ian's bottom lip, pulling it into Jessen's mouth, Ian lost his mind.

He moaned. Loudly.

Jessen responded by grabbing his neck with one hand and slipping the other up into his hair to fist it, making his scalp tingle.

He pressed a quick succession of kisses onto Ian's eager mouth before tracing the seam of his lips with the tip of his wicked tongue.

Ian had never...had *never*. The sensation went straight to his cock, and he shuddered, every nerve ending on high alert.

"Jesus, Ian." Jessen panted, his eyes dark and wild. His hands gripped Ian like he was afraid he'd disappear. "Where did you come from?"

"Roxborough."

Jessen shook his head. "Come here."

He maneuvered him until Ian found himself on his knees straddling Jessen's lap.

Jessen took his mouth again, sucking on his bottom lip until he thought he might come in his jeans.

Ian was hard, harder than he'd ever been, and needy. So damn needy.

He whimpered when Jessen kissed across his jawline and down his neck, latching onto the sensitive skin at his collar and groaning like it was the best thing he'd ever tasted.

"What are you…?" Ian lost his language when Jessen began to suck. Hard. "Ohhhfuck."

The delicate, long fingers than Ian had admired as they coaxed music out of a guitar now held his ass in a tight grip, and Jessen pulled Ian closer until their bodies were flush.

"Oh, God."

Jessen was hard too, and he bucked up between Ian's spread legs.

"Oh…God!"

Ian's cock throbbed, and he didn't know what to do. A tiny, helpless sound escaped his throat.

Jessen took mercy and detached himself from Ian's skin. "Fuck, I'm sorry, fuck…"

He leaned back, putting a small amount of distance between them, but Ian was floored by the state of him.

Flushed cheeks, blown pupils, shiny, swollen mouth. He was a fucking wet dream.

Jessen's hands gripped Ian's hips like a vise.

"Are you real?"

The blond blinked a few times. He looked dazed. "What, baby?"

"Never mind."

"Hey." Jessen tipped Ian's chin up again with one finger. "I'm sorry, okay? I got a little carried away. It's just…you're…you're so…" He shook his head.

"I'm so what?"

Instead of answering, Jessen leaned in for another kiss and Ian met him halfway.

This time, when Jessen's tongue touched his lips, Ian parted them. He heard a gasp, and then his world narrowed down to the feel of another man's tongue gently probing his mouth.

Ian was so caught up in the kiss, he didn't care about the sounds he made. Little whimpers and moans that Jessen seemed to drink down as he pressed further.

He pulled Ian into him and wrapped his arms around his back, sliding one hand up into his hair again.

Ian wound his around Jessen's neck, and felt like he'd always been there. Pressed up against him. The world on fire.

Jessen's hips were insistent, and Ian moved with him, but he was dangerously close to losing it.

He broke away, panting. "Jessen, wait."

"What is it?" He kissed along Ian's jawline until he reached that spot on his neck again, the one that was now overly sensitive.

Ian's breath hitched when his cock pulsed against his zipper, screaming for release.

"I-I...we should..."

Jessen leaned back. "What's wrong?"

Ian couldn't stop squirming, couldn't stop rocking against him. It was the friction. It felt so fucking good.

He didn't know how to articulate this, but Jessen seemed to understand.

His gaze dropped to Ian's fly and back up. "Has anyone ever... touched you?"

Ian froze.

He wanted this.

He wanted it so bad. Wanted this man's fingers on him, wanted a whole hell of a lot more, but...

"We don't have to do anything you don't want to do, Ian. Okay?" Jessen took his face into his hands and brushed his thumbs over his cheeks. "No pressure."

Ian blinked, his head spinning. "Are you real?"

Jessen smiled. It was almost sad. "I'm real, pet."

He pecked him on the lips, and Ian's eyes fluttered closed.

"Look at me."

He did, lost again in the fathomless blue.

"You're safe with me."

"I know."

Jessen seemed relieved. "Yeah?"

Ian nodded.

"Tell me what you want."

Ian exhaled a frustrated groan. "I...I don't know what I want, that's the problem. I don't know...anything."

A look of understanding passed over Jessen's face. He nodded, then moved his hand to Ian's waist, his thumb playing along the seam of his fly.

"Do you want me to touch you?"

Ian squeezed his eyes shut and nodded.

"Use your words, Ian."

"Yes. Touch me." He jumped when Jessen popped open his button.

"Breathe."

The sound of his zipper sliding down was loud, and Ian held his breath despite Jessen's command. He sucked in his stomach when Jessen's knuckles grazed his length over his briefs.

"Wet for me already," the blond husked, and Ian opened his eyes to look down, mortified by the dark spot on the front of his underwear.

Then Jessen brushed his thumb over the tip of Ian's dick, and he forgot to care about noises or wet spots or whether he'd put on a clean pair. He was fairly certain he had.

When those long fingers crept into his briefs and wrapped themselves around his aching flesh, Ian thought he just might pass out.

He dropped his forehead to Jessen's shoulder and moaned helplessly.

"*Fy faen.*" Jessen sounded wrecked. His strokes were slow at first, testing Ian. Then his grip grew firmer, more purposeful.

It didn't really matter, Ian was seconds from coming all over him.

He raised his head to warn him.

"I'm gonna..."

Jessen gripped his hair and attacked his mouth like a man

possessed, drawing out low moans that matched his own feral growls.

Ian's hips rocked as he fucked up into Jessen's hand, unable to stop himself.

Jessen pumped harder, faster.

"Come, baby." He panted against Ian's lips. "Come for me. Shit."

Ian nearly blacked out when the first viscous rope shot from his body. He threw his head back, a long, low moan emanating from his throat.

"Shit, oh shit...look at you. Shit." Jessen babbled while Ian's soul poured out of his dick in thick spurts against Jessen's now-ruined t-shirt. A vintage Ramones no less.

Ian shook and came and panted and whimpered and it was... amazing. Incredible. Perfect.

Chapter 10

Ian wasn't sure how long he sat with his head on Jessen's shoulder, but he gradually became aware of two things. The rock hard erection that had been pressing against the inside of his thigh was gone, and Jessen was trembling with laughter.

At first, Ian thought he was laughing at him. He sat up, ready to defend himself.

"What's so funny?"

"Oh, baby…"

Jessen grabbed the hem of his soiled tee and whipped it over his head. It landed somewhere in the corner of Ian's room. Then he wrapped his arms around Ian and pulled him into a hug.

His mind snagged on the fact that Jessen was now half-naked and that he was holding him like he mattered.

"What about you?"

"Hmm?" Jessen's voice had taken on a dreamy quality.

Ian leaned back and let his gaze flick down to Jessen's groin. "Aren't you…I mean, don't you wanna…?"

Jessen splayed a hand over Ian's cheek, his expression fond. "Already taken care of."

"Huh?"

Jessen started to laugh again and the penny dropped for Ian.

His eyes went wide. "You…?"

"Came in my pants like a pubescent teen? Yep. You did that to me, young Ian."

He frowned. "Don't call me that. Not after…just don't. Okay?"

Jessen sobered, nodding once. "Okay."

Ian allowed Jessen to pull him close, relishing the warm, hard press of his muscles against his own chest.

"Can I take my shirt off too?"

"Why are you asking?"

Ian sat up. "I don't know the protocol here."

Jessen chuckled, reaching up to brush the hair back from Ian's eyes.

"The protocol is you do what feels good."

"I think having your skin against my skin would feel good."

He smiled. "I think so too."

Together, they removed Ian's hoodie and then his t-shirt.

Jessen wasted no time pulling Ian back into his arms, and it felt incredible. Warm skin against warm skin. Toned muscle against toned muscle. It felt the way Ian always thought it would, only better.

"Better?" Jessen's voice echoed Ian's thoughts and had taken on a deeper timbre that made his skin hum.

"Mmm, better."

Jessen's arms tightened around him as if holding him was an imperative. A need.

Ian had never had that, had never been held like that. He had never shared himself in that way. Had never had anyone who wanted to just hold him.

"Ian?"

"Yeah?"

"Can I stay tonight?" Jessen sounded almost shy. "We can cuddle like this, nothing more if that's what you want, I just…"

Ian raised his head and met Jessen's gaze. "Please stay."

Jessen smiled, his blue eyes twinkling, and pecked him on the lips.

They stood slowly and stripped down to their underwear.

Ian had to lend Jessen a clean pair and turned around to give him privacy when he changed, which made Jessen laugh. Then they climbed into his too-small-for-two-guys-over-six-feet bed.

Once again, Ian found himself wrapped up in Jessen's arms.

He fit his thigh over one of the taller man's legs. There was more skin, more heat, just more of everything and Ian was overwhelmed. They lay in the cool sheets and the dark night, the only sound in the room their mingled breaths.

Jessen traced lazy circles over Ian's back with smooth fingertips.

"Do you like it?" Ian whispered because it seemed like he should.

"Like what?"

"The touring and stuff."

Jessen shifted under him, distributing Ian's weight so he was partially on his side. He turned his face toward him.

"Sometimes." His gaze drifted to the ceiling. "Sometimes no."

"You're good."

He smiled. "Thanks."

"I mean it." Ian propped himself up on his elbow so he could peer down at Jessen.

The blond smiled. "I know you do, thanks."

Ian frowned. "Don't dismiss the compliment."

"I'm not."

"Yes, you are. Is it because of Mattias?"

Jessen's lips twitched. "Matty is the star of the family."

Feeling brave, Ian reached down and grabbed one of Jessen's hands, bringing it to his mouth. He kissed each of the long, slender fingers. When he met Jessen's gaze again, the other man looked amazed. Entranced.

"Your hands are incredible," Ian explained when Jessen flicked his eyebrows in question. "I watched you play tonight and I...I couldn't take my eyes off you. And your voice..."

"You like my voice?" Jessen turned his wrist and placed the hand on Ian's cheek.

Ian nodded, closing his eyes. "You have a gift, Jess. Mattias or no Mattias, you have a gift."

He heard and felt him exhale. "Jessen."

"Hmm?" Ian opened his eyes.

"Call me Jessen. I like it that you do. Jacob and Matty call me Jess, you…you I want to call me Jessen."

Ian searched his face and saw a need there, more than physical, a spiritual need. He nodded.

"Jessen."

The blond leaned up and kissed him, his tongue lapping at Ian's lips right away.

Ian opened for him, let Jessen drag him down until he was on his back and breathing hard.

Jessen hovered, braced on his arms which flexed beautifully. Muscles carved from the finest marble.

"Fuck, Ian…" He looked drugged.

"What…?"

Jessen dropped his head to Ian's chest, and he took the opportunity to slip his fingers into all that fine, blond hair. He massaged Jessen's scalp and was rewarded with a satisfying groan.

"I should go," he said, his voice full of gravel.

Panic rose in Ian's chest, and his hands stilled. "Why?"

"Because, if I stay, we may end up doing something you'll regret in the morning."

Oh.

"Like what?"

Jessen lifted his head enough to meet Ian's eyes. His were dark, nearly black, and Ian felt the evidence of his warning hard and insistent against his hip.

His own cock tented his boxer briefs.

The blond nodded toward it. "I want to get my mouth around that."

His gaze raked up Ian's body like he wanted to eat him alive. When he finally met Ian's eyes, he must have seen the terror in them. His expression softened.

"Only if you say so."

"I...yes." He was in danger of shaking the flesh from his bones, but Ian wanted it. Needed it.

Jessen leaned down and kissed him, and it was sweet. Hot. Full of promises.

He knelt between Ian's legs, using his knees to press them wider. When his hand went to the waistband of Ian's underwear, Ian had to fight to keep his eyes open.

"I have to admit, knowing I'll be the first to do this is a bit of a thrill."

"Is that why you want to do it?"

Jessen's gaze flicked up to Ian's and back down to where his hands worked the elastic over his hips.

"No." He eased the fabric down, and Ian's cock sprang free, embarrassingly hard and already leaking. "I want to because you are sexy as fuck and you don't even know it."

Ian lifted his ass as Jessen divested him of the briefs.

"I want to do it because I can't think of anything I want more right now than to make you come again."

Ian was mesmerized watching Jessen's gaze drink him in like he was a piece of art. Or a premium steak. As strange as it felt to be the object of a virtual stranger's desire, Ian enjoyed every second of Jessen's attention.

Feeling bold, he raised his arms above his head and arched his back a bit.

Jessen growled.

"Do that again."

Ian repeated the movement, watching from under hooded eyes. He felt powerful. Until Jessen wrapped those beautiful fingers of his around him again.

"Hold onto something," he warned before sliding down between Ian's thighs, using his wide shoulders to hold him open. "You're beautiful, Ian."

Before he could respond, the tip of his dick was surrounded by wet, scorching heat. His hips jack-knifed off the bed and Jessen had to pin him down.

"Breathe, baby. I've got you." He licked a line up one side of his cock and down the other, humming like he'd just discovered the best flavor of ice cream ever invented before taking Ian into his mouth.

Breathing was not an option.

Thinking was not an option.

Ian fisted the sheets in both hands and tried to keep his brain from melting out of his ears.

Holy *fuck!*

Is this what he had been missing?

He thought back to the few attempts at blowing him he'd thwarted, by a few girls he'd made out with at parties, and wondered if it would have felt the same if he'd let them.

The answer came right away.

No.

Impossible.

Jessen's mouth was perfect. And then it left him with a pop.

"You okay?"

"I didn't know." Air was a luxury as Ian sputtered and gasped.

One slender hand stroked him, slow and gentle.

"Didn't know what, babe?"

"This. I didn't know this." Ian peered down between his legs and almost came just from the sight of the gorgeous blond with his mouth on him.

Jessen lifted his head and flashed a wicked smile. "You don't know anything yet."

There was heat and pressure and sound and mind-blowing pleasure. Ian was in danger of having a real out-of-body experience as Jessen worked him over, eliciting noises Ian didn't know he was capable of making.

"Fuck, Jessen..."

The man growled. "God, I love the way that sounds coming out of that pretty mouth of yours."

Ian wasn't going to last and, oh, how he wanted to last. He wanted the moment, the whole night, to stretch out forever.

Jessen's hands weren't idle.

He stroked Ian's flesh, squeezed his thighs encouragingly, and coaxed them wider. He nuzzled Ian's balls, licking and sucking them.

Ian hadn't even known that was a thing.

"Gonna make you come so hard."

"Please."

Fingers danced along the expanding crack of his ass, and Ian tensed.

Jessen stopped and looked up. His face was flush, his eyes glassy as he met Ian's watery gaze.

"Trust me?"

"Yes." Ian didn't hesitate.

"Do you have lube?"

The breath wheezed from his lungs. "I…"

"I'm not going to fuck you, Ian." Jessen petted his aching cock. "I just want to make you feel good. Trust me, I would never…"

"I know." Ian exhaled slowly. "The drawer there."

He nodded to Jessen's left and took advantage of the momentary reprieve, taking deep gulps of air while he could.

Jessen stretched over and opened the drawer. "Yes," he hissed. "This is the good stuff."

"I use it for…um…you know."

The blond grinned. "Now *that* I would like to see sometime."

The thought of having Jessen's eyes on him while he jerked-off did crazy things to Ian's libido. His cock twitched, pulsing a drop of pre-come that slithered down its length.

"I think you like that," Jessen teased.

Ian heard the telltale click of the bottle and tensed.

"Shhh." Jessen cooed. "Nothing but pleasure, I promise."

His fingertips, a little cold from the lube, slid along Ian's crease and Ian tried to breathe through the foreign sensation. Mercifully, Jessen resumed his exploration of Ian's dick.

As soon as he was surrounded by that wet heat, the fear melted away. He didn't notice how close Jessen was to his hole until something brushed over it.

He hissed.

"Easy, I'm just touching you."

It wasn't unpleasant, exactly, just unfamiliar.

"I know it feels odd. Tell me if you want me to stop, okay?"

Ian nodded, his head digging down into the pillow. Damp clumps of his hair clung to his forehead, but he couldn't be bothered to brush them away.

Jessen's mouth went around him again, his tongue doing wicked things that Ian never wanted to end. And then he was *there*, his finger in a place Ian himself had never dared to touch, except with a bar of soap and a washcloth.

He let out a slow breath and let the feeling wash over him. The suction on his cock, the pressure on his ass. The combination was heady.

In the distance, he heard the clock tower chime midnight and then Jessen breached him. Just the tip of a finger as he took a long pull on his cock, but it was enough.

Ian came hard, groaning and growling while the chimes sounded, ushering in yet another birthday. Though this one he would surely remember.

Stars burst behind his eyes, and his body seized up with the pleasure.

Before he could come down from his high, Jessen had covered him. Animalistic sounds poured out of his long, ivory throat.

He lined up his cock with the crook of Ian's thigh and rutted against him, landing open-mouthed kisses all along Ian's chest, neck, and face.

Ian turned his head and let Jessen claim his mouth, tasting himself on the other man's tongue. His aftershocks were brutal, intensified by the rhythmic thrusts.

He wrapped his arms around Jessen's back and spread his legs wider. His balls were sensitive, and the friction hurt, but he was determined.

"Come for me, Jessen," he rasped.

"Ah, fuck...Ian...*faen, du er jævla deilig.*"

Jessen groaned into his neck, liquid heat splashing across Ian's abdomen and side while he panted into his hair. They were a sticky, sweaty mess and Ian had never, ever been so happy.

The pair lay heavy-limbed and breathing hard for long minutes.

"Towel?" Jessen's after-sex voice was decadent.

"There's one on the back of my desk chair."

The bed shifted as he got up and the chilled air hit Ian's slick skin like ice water. He shivered.

"Hang on, baby." Jessen gently cleaned him up and then tended to himself.

Ian was struck with a sudden panic, a sense of loss. Jessen would probably leave and Ian wasn't ready to let him go, not yet.

He steeled himself for the inevitable goodbye, but Jessen surprised him yet again.

"Let's get under the duvet."

Ian shifted over, and Jessen laid down next to him, gathering him close to his chest as soon as he settled.

"This okay?"

Ian nodded into Jessen's neck. He could barely keep his eyes open.

"Sleep." Jessen kissed his forehead. "I'll be here when you wake up."

"Why?" Ian managed to mumble before succumbing.

"Nowhere else I'd rather be."

Chapter 11

Ian woke to the smell of burning sugar. Cracking one eye open, he realized it was still nighttime.

His desk lamp had been turned on, and beside it stood a very naked Norwegian, his ass on full display while he muttered curses under his breath.

"What are you doing?"

"Good morning!" Jessen looked over his shoulder, his smile bright and his eyebrows up somewhere under the curls that hung over his forehead.

Ian glanced at his watch. "It's three a.m."

"Did I wake you? I didn't mean to yet, I was just hungry." Jessen turned back to whatever he was doing, whatever was making that godawful smell. "Forgot to eat dinner, and you had these toaster pastries. And a toaster."

Ian slipped out of bed and padded over to the desk where Jessen had cleared a space and plugged in the appliance.

"I thought it was busted."

"The spring was dislodged. I fixed it. And I was going to surprise you with this gourmet meal of..." Jessen lifted the box of sugary cardboard. "Frosted blueberry delight."

A wisp of smoke curled out of the top of the toaster.

"Is it burning?"

Jessen shook his head. "No, I think there are bits in the bottom. You should clean this from time to time."

"I never use it."

Jessen looked at him and frowned. "Then how do you warm your pastries?"

Ian shrugged. "Since I thought it was broken, I got used to eating them cold."

The blond made a face like a two-year-old. "Blech. That's pitiful."

Jessen turned back to the contraption, presumably monitoring it in case it went up in flames.

Ian took the opportunity to glance down at Jessen's ass. It was nice. Firm but softly rounded. He had the overwhelming urge to cup it in his hand but shut it down.

Sure, they were standing naked in his dorm room waiting for frosted carbs to burn, but he didn't know the protocol. He'd half expected to wake up alone, despite Jessen's promise.

When he looked up, Jessen's blue gaze was on him again.

"Hi," he said in a voice so soft it gave Ian chills. Jessen frowned. "Are you cold?"

Ian shook his head, not trusting his voice.

Jessen smiled and then wrapped an arm around Ian's waist, pulling him in tight. He dropped a soft kiss on Ian's forehead and met his eyes, his full of something Ian couldn't name.

"Hi," he said again, just as quietly as before.

"Hi." Ian didn't know what to do with his hands. He didn't know what to do period.

"How do you feel?"

Jessen stroked Ian's skin ever-so-lightly. Not in a sexual way, but it was tender. Confusing.

"I'm fine, I think."

"Good."

The toaster popped and Ian jumped, causing Jessen to chuckle.

The blond let him go and retrieved the pastries from the metal slot with the tips of his fingers. He hissed.

"Careful." Ian ripped a paper towel off the roll he kept on his desk and held it out for Jessen to place the toasted goods onto it.

"E, voila!" Jessen did so with a flourish. "Breakfast is served."

Ian laughed. He couldn't help it The guy was funny and charming. And sweet. And hot as hell.

They climbed back into his bed, thankfully pulling the duvet up to cover critical parts, and spread the pastries between them. There were three.

"We'll split the third one, okay? Unless you're super hungry."

"No, that's fair." Ian picked it up and broke it into approximate halves, handing one of them to Jessen.

"*Takk.*"

"Is that 'thank you' in Norwegian?"

Jessen nodded around a mouthful. "Mmm hmm."

"Do you miss Oslo?"

"I do, and I don't." Jessen finished his half and reached for his whole tart. "It's small, so everyone knows everyone. It can feel claustrophobic."

"It's a big city, though. Isn't it?"

"It is, but..." Jessen ran a hand back through his hair, and Ian tracked the movement.

He loved the way the curls submitted for only an instant before reasserting themselves in any way they chose. He got the feeling Jessen was much the same.

"In the music scene, in any creative scene really, the pool is small. So, everyone knows what everyone else is doing. It can be very..."

"Competitive?"

"Yeah, that's one word for it." Jessen chewed thoughtfully. "Don't get me wrong, I love Oslo. Love it. But I'm kinda glad I don't live there right now."

"You think you will again someday?"

"Definitely. It's beautiful, and the people are amazing. You'd love it." He smiled around another bite.

"You think so?" Ian finished off his first half.

"Absolutely, and they'd love you." Jessen's smile made Ian's chest tight. There was so much in it, so much affection and invitation.

Ian dropped his gaze to his food. "Thanks for breakfast."

"Anytime."

They finished their meal in silence, though Ian's mind raced. He searched for things to say, interesting topics to bring up, but nothing seemed appropriate.

Really, all he wanted to do was stare at Jessen. Watch Jessen move and breathe and just be. He was bewildered by how beautiful the guy was, even more so that he was there with him. In Ian's room, in Ian's bed.

"Could I ask you a question?" Jessen sat lotus style and faced him.

Ian tried not to think of the long, thickness that hung between his legs just under the covers.

"Um, sure."

"You're a good-looking guy."

Ian snorted.

Jessen frowned. "What was that?"

"Nothing, I just…I know what I look like and those aren't the words I'd apply."

His eyes narrowed. "What words would you apply, then?"

Ian thought for a moment because this was not something that had ever come up for him before. No one had ever complimented his looks, and he was just fine with it. It wasn't like he spent any time worrying about his appearance.

Sure, it would be nice to be as effortlessly gorgeous as the Sørensen twins, but he was sure there was a certain set of pressures that came along with it.

More pressure was not something Ian needed.

"Functional," Ian answered after a moment or two. "Passable. Like, I won't scare children on the street or anything."

Jessen moved forward so swiftly Ian had to balance himself on his hands. The blond loomed over him, hovering an inch away from his face, and his gaze locked on Ian's mouth.

"Is that why you spend your Saturday nights curled up with your books? Because you think you're *passable*?"

"I…"

Jessen closed his eyes and leaned in, touching his nose to Ian's and dragging it along its length.

Ian's eyes fluttered shut because this…this was more intimate than anything they had done so far.

He continued to brush his perfect nose over Ian's cheeks, first one then the other, over and over until Ian felt drugged.

Slowly, Jessen leaned forward, forcing Ian to move until he was on his back. The blond settled at his side and brought a hand up to Ian's cheek, his thumb caressing him.

"You're gorgeous, Ian," Jessen whispered against his lips before kissing him gently. "Absolutely fucking gorgeous, and lovely, and just…sweet. You're so goddamn sweet."

Ian shuddered. "Thanks?"

Jessen chuckled, pulling back enough to look down at him. "Was that a question?"

"No, I mean…thanks for…the words are nice."

"You think they're just words?"

Ian shrugged one shoulder. "Look, let's be honest with each other, okay?"

Jessen nodded. "Okay."

"You're here because you wanted to get laid, and I was very clearly into you."

"Was?"

"Am." Ian felt his cheeks warm but pushed through anyway. "I'm not delusional. You're a rock guy, and your adrenaline is pumping, you needed a release, and I was convenient."

Jessen reeled back as if he'd been struck. "Wow."

Ian turned to face him, suddenly unsure. "I meant no offense."

The other man laughed.

"Really? You just called me a ho. Not that there's anything wrong with being a ho, but I'd like to have earned the title rather than have it thrust upon me."

Ian winced. "Shit, I'm sorry. I didn't mean it like that."

Jessen shook his head and then reached for him, pulling Ian closer as he laid on his back.

"Young Ian, I'm here with you because I was into you too. *Am* into you. You're not a notch on my proverbial belt. Don't believe everything you read about the rock and roll lifestyle. Most of it is spent on tour vans and buses, or in airport lounges and dingy, no-name hotel rooms. I don't make it a habit of hooking up after every gig."

"Some, though?"

Jessen nodded and carded his hand through Ian's hair. "A few, but never like this. Never like…you."

He leaned over and touched their lips together.

"Oh."

Jessen smiled. "Yeah, oh."

⬜

"FIRST KISS?"

"Ingrid Hahn when I was nine. It was awful."

Ian lay in Jessen's arms while he trailed those glorious, long fingers over his skin. Goosebumps raced along after his fingertips and Ian watched Jessen as he watched them erupt and fade. Over and over.

Christ, Jessen was beautiful. Long, fair lashes batted against his high cheekbones.

Ian wanted to keep him. He wanted to keep him so fucking bad.

"I think first kisses are supposed to suck."

"Did yours?"

Ian nodded against Jessen's shoulder. "The worst."

"Girl?"

"Yeah."

"That probably had something to do with it," Jessen said, chuckling. "Have you always known you were gay?"

Ian looked up and met his gaze. "No. Have you always known you were bi?"

"Pan."

"Really?"

Jessen smiled into Ian's wide eyes.

"Yep. And I've probably always known, I mean, pretty is pretty. Hot is hot." He ran the pad of his finger across Ian's lips, causing his breath to hitch. Again. "You have the prettiest mouth I've ever seen. It's like…a cupid's bow."

He blushed, caught in Jessen's gaze.

"And your eyes…so green. Like springtime."

Ian's heart thumped hard against his ribcage. He laughed nervously. "Now I know who writes those cheesy lyrics for your band."

Jessen chuckled, his mouth quirking to one side. "Guilty."

He stared into Ian's eyes for so long Ian's breathing stuttered.

"I really want to kiss you," Jessen whispered into their bubble of intimacy.

"What's stopping you?"

In the distance, the clock tower chimed five a.m.

"I'm afraid if I do, I'll never want to leave."

"You have to, though."

"I know." Jessen kissed him.

It was a soft brushing of lips, so tender Ian whimpered.

Jessen groaned and touched the tip of his tongue to Ian's bottom lip, kissing him over and over with just that hint of it.

Bracing himself on his side, one arm across the pillow above Ian's head, the other draped across his abdomen, Jessen nipped at him. The tightening and relaxing of his fingers at Ian's waist was the only thing that betrayed how affected he was.

Everything else was simple. Lazy. They lay side-by-side, only their upper bodies touching.

It was almost innocent.

Ian was in real danger of losing more than his BJ virginity.

He'd never experienced anything like this before and wasn't sure how he was supposed to let it go now that he had.

"Fuck," Jessen mumbled, dropping his head to the pillow beside Ian's.

"What's wrong?"

"I don't know how I'm going to walk out the door and get back on the bus." He lifted up and stared down at Ian, searching his face. "I wish I could take you with me."

"You could always stay here," Ian joked. "Play in the Hub."

"I could."

Ian laughed, but Jessen didn't.

"Mattias doesn't need me, not really. It's him they're cheering for every night."

Ian frowned. "That's not true."

"It is. I could stop all this, all the travel and the bullshit, and just…stay in Philly. Or at least New York. It's not far. I could see you four, five times a week."

"You're talking nonsense, Jessen." Ian laughed but it sounded amazing, perfect really, and totally nuts.

"I'd do it, though. For you."

"You barely know me," Ian scoffed, his heart sputtering.

"I *want* to know you, though. Don't you understand? I want to get to know you. I-I feel like…this, whatever this is, it feels like it could…" He exhaled, studying Ian's face. "Don't you feel it, too?"

He did. Of course, he did, but this wasn't some fairy tale.

Jessen nodded sharply. "I'm staying."

"No."

"Yes, because if this is what I think it is…"

"What do you think it is?" Ian held his breath.

Jessen's gaze softened. He trailed his fingers across Ian's cheek.

"I'm pretty sure I'm going to fall in love with you."

Jesus.

He kissed him, nuzzling his nose against Ian's cheek again. It felt so natural.

"*Faen*, I'm halfway there already, and it's only been a few hours." He met Ian's startled gaze. "Tell me you feel it too, young Ian. Ian." *Kiss.* "Ian." *Kiss.* "Ian…tell me I'm not alone here."

"You're not," Ian whispered, afraid he'd wake up any minute and find it was all a fever dream.

Jessen kissed him again.

Held him through the night. Promised him the moon.

Showed him more stars.

When Ian did wake in the morning, Jessen was gone. A note on the desk and a few crumbs of pastry were the only evidence he'd ever been there. That and Ian's fluttering heart.

Text me. We're in D.C. tonight.

J

212.555.1341

Plugging Jessen into his contacts, Ian fired off a text.

IAN: Be safe
   JESSEN: Thanks, babe! I'll see you soon.

ALL DAY, Ian floated on clouds. He replayed their night together over and over in his head, trying to hold onto every little detail.

He'd never felt so wanted before, so cherished. And he missed Jessen. So much.

Still, he walked around campus with a big ass grin. And whenever anyone asked him about it, Ian just shrugged and grinned even more.

By the time night fell, Ian was exhausted. He fell into his bed and was out like a light instantly.

It seemed like he'd only been asleep for a few seconds when someone knocked at his door. A quick glance at his watch told him it was after one in the morning.

Ian opened the door and was immediately engulfed in Jessen's arms.

"*Faen,* I missed you so much."

The kiss was frantic. Clothes flew everywhere, and Ian couldn't get him naked fast enough.

"All I could think about was getting to you. I messed up so many of my cues tonight."

"I'm sorry."

"Don't be," Jessen panted as he kicked away his jeans and underwear. "Be sorry for this shitty little city you live in and its godawful public transportation. I couldn't even take a proper train here!"

Ian bristled. "Don't talk about Philly like that. This place is awesome."

"Awesome? You're using this word, but I do not think it means what you think it means."

"Fuck you."

"No," Jessen husked against Ian's skin as he pushed him down. "Fuck you."

Ian writhed on the mattress as Jessen descended upon him. It felt like the man had grown an extra pair of hands. He was everywhere.

"I want you to."

Jessen froze and looked down at Ian. "What?"

Ian took a deep breath and plunged forward. "I want you to fuck me."

He shook his head. "No, baby. Not yet."

Ian frowned. "Why not?"

He kissed him deeply and Ian wrapped his arms around him. "Soon," Jessen whispered. "When we're ready."

⸺

JESSEN: I think I found a job in Philly. I can teach guitar! We're doing this, baby.

    IAN: oxo

IAN STARTED MAKING PLANS. With his scholarship, he didn't need to worry about housing. And he was more than happy to share his space with Jessen if it came down to that.

When Jessen came back two nights later, they barely spoke. He pressed Ian into the mattress and dropped to his knees. The last coherent thought Ian had was that Jessen felt like heaven against his skin.

▭

JESSEN: We need to get a bigger mattress. That little one is a bitch to sleep on, among other things.

IAN: Okay!

HE WAS RIGHT, of course. It wasn't something Ian had ever paid attention to before. It had just been a place to sleep. Not anymore.

JESSEN: Are you obligated to stay on campus? I found this fantastic loft apartment online.

IAN: Yeah?

Ian loved living on campus, but he wasn't married to the idea of staying there. He just wanted to be wherever Jessen was.

▭

IAN WAS awake when Jessen tapped on his door. He jumped up and threw it open, his breath catching at the sight of his wild-haired, wild-eyed lover.

Before Jessen could speak, Ian grabbed him by the collar and attacked his mouth. He was desperately hungry for all the things Jessen could do to him, and he wanted more.

"Tonight. Please."

Jessen panted against his lips, his fingers digging into Ian's sides. "Yeah, okay...yeah. *Faen...*"

Chapter 12

"Fuck."

As Jessen dragged his calloused palms over his heated skin, Ian slowly lost his mind. It was as if the blond wanted to touch him everywhere, all at once.

Jessen nipped at points on his body Ian hadn't known were sensitive.

The area just below his chin.

The V where his arm met his torso.

The smooth skin where his leg connected to his hip.

Every touch, every lick, sent him spiraling.

"I can't...I can't..."

Jessen peered up at him from under his lashes, his eyes dark with lust. "Can't what, baby?"

"Can't take anymore. I need..."

The blond knelt over his prone, naked body and straddled his thighs. His gorgeous cock was on proud display, engorged, shiny at the tip, red like fire, and just as hot to touch as Ian reached up to wrap his hand around it.

Jessen batted him away. "No, this is all about you. Tell me what you need."

"You. I need you."

He stilled and Ian did too, holding his gaze.

They had stayed that way for a long minute before Jessen exhaled and closed his eyes.

Ian noted the slight tremble in his toned frame.

"You're going to be the end of me, young Ian."

Before he could protest the moniker, Jessen unceremoniously dropped down and took his cock into his mouth, punching the breath out of his lungs.

Ian bit back a scream when he felt himself hit the back of the other man's throat. He hummed around him, and Ian's hands flew into his hair.

"Fuck, fuck, stop!" Ian clenched his abs and tried to hold back the orgasm barreling down on him. "Not like this."

Jessen released him and looked up. "Lube. Now."

Ian grabbed it from under the pillow, tossing it down.

He caught it with one hand. "Are you sure?"

"Yes, I'm so sure."

The wicked grin returned. "Spread your legs for me then, baby."

Ian did, and they were shaking. He shook all over, and Jessen smoothed his hands over his skin, trying to relax him. There was no relaxation to be had.

Every tender kiss and loving touch annihilated him. He was falling so hard for this person, this man, and Ian didn't know how to stop it. Wasn't sure if he should.

Jessen leaned forward and kissed him, patiently explored every nook and cranny of his mouth with an expert tongue. The sounds he made, like Ian was the best thing he'd ever tasted, made Ian's head spin. But the kiss was fruitful. He relaxed under the hard body above him.

A hand wrapped around his cock, gently at first, and Ian's breath hitched before he relaxed again. Surrendered to the kisses, the nuzzling, the words of praise.

"You're so beautiful," Jessen rasped.

Ian ran his hands over acres of smooth skin, marveled at the fine blond hairs that blanketed Jessen's chest, barely visible to the naked eye.

"So are you, Jessen."

That earned him a smile and a sigh and a kiss that blew off the top of his head. Ian didn't know where Jessen had learned to kiss like that, but he wanted to send a bouquet to whoever had taught him. It was sweet and filthy all at once.

When Jessen parted Ian's cheeks with his fingers, gently probing his puckered ring, Ian barely gasped. He was ready, so ready.

Jessen raised his head and stared down into Ian's eyes. Then Ian felt him there, his finger slick with wet. He willed himself to relax, to open up.

"We're not in a hurry, Ian," he whispered above him, watching him carefully. There was concern in his expression, along with joy and a little bit of awe.

Ian wondered what he saw, besides the quivering, inexperienced mess that he was. He took a deep breath, let it out slowly, and felt the muscle give.

Jessen's fingertip slipped inside, and it was foreign, but felt so right. He smiled, and Jessen smiled back.

He pecked Ian on the lips and then his chin, worked his way down his neck to Ian's chest and – oh – a quick flick of his tongue across Ian's nipple had him squirming.

All the while, the finger pressed and wiggled, seeking entry. Opening him.

Ian felt himself relax around it, felt his body invite it inside.

Jessen groaned.

"So tight…"

He continued to work his way down Ian's body.

Ian put one arm behind his head, propping it up so he could watch. The other hand went into Jessen's hair, combing gently through the strands until Jessen took the tip of Ian's cock into his mouth.

He fisted that fine, blond hair and moaned, his legs opening wider on their own.

Jessen groaned into his flesh, and Ian suddenly felt full.

He gasped.

"Just adding another finger, baby. Breathe. You're doing so well."

Ian tried, and he was doing well, he thought, until Jessen's breath ghosted across the skin between his cheeks.

"Oh, God, what're you…"

"I want to taste you first."

Warm, wet, soft. Jessen's tongue joined his fingers as they pressed inside him, the dual sensations almost too much to bear.

Ian held his breath instead, afraid he'd scream. It was all too intense for his brain to process.

Jessen pumped his hand, testing him, and Ian couldn't suppress the moan. He felt invaded by the pleasure, though it was laced with pain, Jessen's fingers and tongue taking him to a place he'd never been.

He squeezed his eyes shut and let it surround him, his cock throbbing and leaking against his belly.

"So good," he gasped.

"Yeah?" Jessen pressed gentle kisses to his balls, licked his skin, and sucked it into his perfect mouth.

Ian had to watch. He forced his eyes open so he could.

Blue eyes met his over the rise of his cock and Ian was transfixed.

The fingers pushed and pulled, and Ian saw Jessen twist his wrist, brushing against a spot that finally brought forth the bitten-back scream.

"Ah, there you are," Jessen purred, his fingers making squelching sounds as he moved them.

It was crazy.

Ian was sweating and panting and trying not to come yet while Jessen worked those digits inside him. He felt so full but knew there was more to come. He was so ready for it.

"More."

Three fingers felt like someone had tried to shove a baseball bat up his ass. Ian went rigid with the pain, his back arching.

"Okay," Jessen murmured, easing back. "It's okay, we're going slow."

And he did, so slowly. He twisted and pushed, pulled and coerced Ian's ring of muscle until pleasure won the war.

Ian sighed, relaxing against the mattress. He blinked his eyes open and dared to look down.

The expression on Jessen's face was beatific. "So perfect," he said, his eyes on Ian's.

"Please." It was all Ian could say.

Jessen nodded and climbed to his knees, his fingers still dancing inside him.

"Condom."

Ian was grateful he'd had the forethought to get some, and that they were within reach.

Lifting one heavy arm, he felt around his nightstand for the box, grabbing it and bringing it to his chest. He opened the lid and pulled out a strip tossing the rest to the floor somewhere.

Jessen grabbed the end square, and Ian helped him rip it off. Watched him opened the package with his teeth. Watched him take himself in one hand and roll the latex on in one smooth move, and then pour more lube over his cock until it was glistening, his eyes never leaving Ian's.

It was the sexiest thing Ian had ever seen.

Emptiness followed when Jessen slid his fingers out. He grabbed Ian's hips and lined himself up with his entrance.

Ian felt a flutter of panic seize his heart, his breaths came in short pants and sputters.

"Baby, look at me."

Ian obeyed, meeting Jessen's dark blue gaze.

There was pressure against his hole, gentle but insistent. All the while, Jessen's focus remained on his face.

Ian could see the strain in his jaw and neck as he pushed forward, pushed inside him, pushed past the resistance.

It didn't hurt, not really, it burned. But the burn was a good one, and he welcomed it.

"Push out."

"Huh?"

"Push out, babe." Jessen's gaze dropped to the place where they were joined. Ian did as he'd asked, bearing down, and then…

And then.

And then.

Oh, God, and then.

"Fuuuuuck."

Jessen slid home. Inch by inch, Ian's body sucked him in and, Jesus, it hurt.

Ian hissed and, frowning, Jessen began to pull back.

"No! Don't, just…wait…"

Jessen froze, his muscles straining. His arms shook and his abs tensed. He looked positively dangerous.

Ian knew he wanted to push forward, wanted to bury himself inside him. He wanted it too, but…not yet. Not yet.

"Breathe," he commanded.

"I am fucking breathing!"

Jessen blinked and then laughed. He laughed.

At first, Ian wanted to punch him. He scowled, and Jessen laughed more, the movement jostling his dick. Which was partially buried in Ian's ass.

It wasn't funny, but it was. Ian laughed too.

"Next time I'm fucking you," he groused.

"Promises, promises."

They continued laughing, stuck in a holding pattern of lust and fear and ridiculousness. The more they laughed, the more Jessen slipped inside until he was nearly all the way there.

"Fuck." Ian's eyes snapped shut with a fresh wave of pain.

Immediately, Jessen sobered. "You okay?"

He nodded. "Yeah, don't stop."

Jessen pushed forward and then bottomed out.

They both went still, panting. Ian from the effort of not pushing Jessen away. It was damn uncomfortable, and he felt like he'd been stuffed for slaughter.

Then Jessen moved. Just a little, experimental twist of his hips but it was enough.

Pleasure flooded Ian's body.

He gasped. "Do that again."

Jessen obliged, rotating his hips so his cock hit that wonderful, little button – that hidden treasure – again and again. And again. Again.

"Fuck, Jessen…fuck."

"Good?"

"Oh, fuck."

Ian grabbed for Jessen's shoulders, pulling him down. He needed to feel more of him, wanted all of him.

Jessen snapped his hips, and Ian moaned, pushing his head back into the pillow. The blond took it as an invitation to attack Ian's throat, nipping and licking his skin there. He began to rock into Ian, and Ian squirmed, trying to get closer.

"Jesus, look at you," Jessen panted above him. He dropped his mouth to Ian's and kissed him, all teeth and tongue, like he was trying to eat his way through his face.

It was ridiculous and hot and, fuck, Ian wanted even more.

He widened his legs, wrapping one around Jessen's hip. Or tried to.

Jessen kept snapping his hips, drumming against that spot inside him - thank God for the prostate - until it was almost too much. Too much and not enough.

"I need…"

"I know."

Jessen reached between them and grabbed Ian's dick, stroking it hard and fast in time with his thrusts. Skin flushed, eyes hooded, and mouth swollen, sweat dripped from his forehead onto Ian's lips.

Ian licked it off.

Jessen's eyes widened as he watched, and then he went rigid, growling like a feral cat. Pleasure screwed his face into a contorted mask as he came.

Ian felt the spike of warmth deep inside him, and then his own orgasm hit.

The scream began somewhere in his gut, barreled up his throat and poured out of his mouth. Ian couldn't stop it, could only hold on while his climax rode him. His vision went black as night while he roared.

Jessen brought him back to earth with his hands on his face, kisses on his cheeks, his eyes, his lips. Whispered words of adoration, some in English and others not, but Ian understood. He just couldn't respond.

He could only lay there, as tears formed in the corners of his eyes, and hope he got to keep this, keep him. Keep Jessen.

Jessen, whose hands were shaking as he took Ian's face into his hands. Jessen, whose lips trembled against his when he kissed him. Jessen who held him until they both fell asleep.

IAN WOKE up to a text the next morning.

JESSEN: Big show tonight. I might break the news to Matty after. Wish me luck, babe.

IAN: Wishing you ALL the luck.

Oh, how he wished he could be there for Jessen.

It wasn't going to be an easy conversation. He should have been there to hold his hand. Something.

Throughout the day, Ian tried hard not to picture them living together, but it was impossible when everything Jessen said seemed to suggest they would. Picking out apartments. Telling his brother he wanted to quit the band.

It was happening. It was really happening, and Ian's heart grew three sizes just thinking about it.

He tried to wait up for Jessen, anxious to hear how it went, but fell asleep with the freshly-laundered Ramones tee folded under his cheek.

When Ian blinked his eyes open the next morning and saw the note that had been slipped under his door, he lunged for it.

His heart shattered when he read the two words written in Jessen's lovely script.

I'm sorry.

Chapter 13

Present Day

He could do this.

Ian stood in the hallway outside room 202 and told himself he had this, dammit. Jessen Sørensen was just some guy he used to know. That's all.

Music drifted through the cracks in the door, a soft, mournful tune that tugged at Ian's resolve. He'd have known it was Jessen, even if he hadn't asked Ian to come.

It was the way he played, the way he seduced the instruments he held in those glorious hands of his. Mattias may have been the household name but, for Ian, Jessen was the gifted one. The ethereal one. The angelic one.

Of course, Ian had nearly passed out when he learned there were two of them, two Nordic gods wandering the earth among the mortals.

No.

No.

Jessen was *not* a god. Jessen was a man. Just a man.

A man who looked like a god.

Fucked like a god.

Tasted like Heaven.

And left Hell in his wake.

But a man, nonetheless.

Ian stretched his neck, left then right, rolled his shoulders and raised his hand to knock on the door.

It opened, and there he was, face to face with his past. A past that beamed at him. Beamed. Jessen's eyes shone, and his smile was blinding before he tempered it.

"I was beginning to think you weren't coming."

"I wasn't going to."

Jessen nodded, a tiny version of his smile returning. "I'm glad you did."

He held the door open and gestured Ian inside.

Gray Berber carpet lined the floor and the walls, which Ian assumed was added to insulate the sound. In a building filled with practicing musicians it would have to be essential. If not for privacy, then for sanity.

One large window filled the far wall in the small, rectangular room. On the left sat an upright piano, and in the middle of the space stood a single chair. Jessen's guitar leaned against the piano's bench.

"Cozy," Ian offered, taking a seat on the bench.

"I like it here. I can come at any hour and find others working in some of the other rooms." He sat in the chair, which was a little too close to Ian for comfort. Their knees bumped, and Ian flinched.

Jessen froze for a moment and then scooted his chair back an inch.

"Better?"

"Thanks."

Ian made a show of inspecting the piano keys. The Steinway was old, maybe a hundred years, but it was in pretty good shape. He splayed his thumb and pinkie over several keys, counting eight between them.

"That's quite a range," Jessen said. "You play?"

Ian plucked one key, noting how the room all but absorbed any reverberation. "No."

He turned and faced Jessen, but kept his eyes on the window. Outside, one of the campus' ancient oak trees stood like a sentinel. He shrugged.

"Chopsticks. That's about it."

He heard Jessen chuckle. "I bet you know more. Twinkle, Twinkle, Little Star, maybe? Alouette?"

Against his will, Ian smiled and shook his head.

"Pity. You have such long, lovely fingers. They were made to play."

Ian cleared his throat because the compliment meant more than it should.

"So…"

Jessen straightened. "Right. As I explained, I have this new piece."

"And you want me to listen?"

"I need you to listen."

It was Jessen's tone that made Ian finally look at him. Once he did, he couldn't look away.

Jessen stared, and Ian stared right back, transported to the first time he saw him. So many years ago.

The hair was different, but the eyes were the same blue. Clear skies blue. Pristine lake blue. His blue. And Jessen spoke volumes with them.

Ian swallowed, wishing he'd brought a bottle of water. Or tequila.

"Play."

Jessen nodded and picked up his guitar. It was an acoustic, blond wood with ivory inlays. He perched it on one knee and hugged it to his body like a lover.

The temperature in the room shot up a few degrees.

The first few notes had the same mournful feel Ian had heard when he stood in the hall. Jessen closed his eyes, those full lashes like dark gold slashes against his pale cheeks.

Ian could watch him when he wasn't looking. It was easier somehow.

Then the music began to speak to him.

Loneliness and loss, triumph and joy, regret. It was all there. Like Jessen had woven his soul into the piece, his life story had been woven into every passing note.

Ian heard laughter in the trills, and longing in the bass notes. Passion in the arpeggios. Lust in the chord progression.

He shivered.

Jessen, eyes closed, his body rocking with the rhythm of the music, was naked before him. May as well have been.

It was beautiful. And really fucking unfair.

"Stop."

The sudden silence was oppressive.

Jessen opened his eyes, blinking slowly as if just waking up from a dream.

"Don't like it?"

Ian took a breath. "Jess, why am I here? What do you want from me? Why...? What the fuck am I supposed to take from this?"

"You don't like it."

"Fuck." Ian ran a rough hand over his face. "Of course I like it, it's fucking gorgeous. It's you! It's..."

Jessen smiled.

"Don't smile at me like that."

"Why not?" His smile grew wider.

Ian looked back at the window. "Because you're not playing fair."

Jessen set the guitar aside and slid out of his chair. On his knees, he shuffled forward until he stopped in front of him. One hand on each thigh, he spread Ian's legs and scooted closer.

Ian reared back as far as he could, which was only as far as the piano. His breaths quickened.

"What are you doing?"

"Something I should have done seven years ago."

"Don't."

"Just...listen. Okay?" Jessen searched his face. He must have taken Ian's silence as affirmation because he continued.

"Do you think it's possible to meet someone before you're meant to?"

Ian tried to tune out the feel of Jessen's thumbs kneading the muscles of his thighs.

"I'm not even sure what that means."

"I was twenty-two when we met."

"And I was twenty."

"Nineteen," Jessen protested.

"The night we met, yes, but...I turned twenty the next morning."

Jessen's hands stilled. He sat back on his heels. "Fuck, are you... are you serious? It was your fucking birthday?"

Ian shrugged. "Yeah."

"Ian," he breathed, a pained expression on his face. "Why didn't you tell me?"

"Does it matter?"

Jessen huffed out an incredulous laugh. "It matters. *You* matter."

"I didn't, though. Not so much."

"*Faen*, Ian..." Jessen ran his hands through his hair. "I know I fucked up. Okay? I know it. You've haunted me for seven fucking years. I know what we had, what we could have had. What we...have."

"What we have?" Ian snorted. "We don't have anything. I don't know you anymore, not that I ever really did. And you sure as hell don't know me."

The blond narrowed his eyes. "What did the piece say to you?"

"Huh?"

"What did you hear?"

"I..." Too much to put into words, that was what. Ian scrambled for something to say.

"Honesty, remember? We said we'd be honest."

"I heard sorrow, regret...happiness, success..."

Jessen nodded, encouraging him. "Yes. Go on."

Ian squirmed in his seat. He dropped his gaze to his lap, feeling all of nineteen again.

"There was loss. And...and love."

"Yes," Jessen whispered.

"But..."

"But?"

"What am I supposed to do with a piece of music, Jessen?"

"It's just a surrogate, Ian. I needed it to reach you so that I could."

"Why?"

He smiled. "You know why."

"No. I don't. I'm done guessing, Jess. I'm done waiting. I'm done pining. I'm just done. Either you tell me what you want, or I am gone."

Jessen bit his lip. His lashes fluttered and he took a breath. "Do you still love me?"

Ian laughed. "What the fuck kind of question is that?"

"That night, after Siv's party, you said…"

He groaned. "I know what I said. And I shouldn't have said it."

"Was it the truth?" Jessen looked so hopeful, so ardently hopeful.

Ian hesitated before nodding. "Yeah, but that doesn't mean anything."

Jessen exhaled a weighted breath. "It means everything to me."

"Why should I care what it means to you, Jess? Really, tell me why?"

Jessen sat up, lifted his hand towards Ian's hair, hovering just over it.

"I've only been in love once, young Ian, and I threw it away for a chance at something I didn't even want. I followed my brother's dream and left mine in a dorm room in Philadelphia."

"Don't bullshit me."

"I'm not, baby." Jessen closed the distance, threading his hand into Ian's unruly locks.

He tried not to react, really he did, but the sigh escaped his throat anyway.

Fuck. He'd missed this man.

"I love you, Ian."

"No, you don't."

"Yes, I do."

Jessen moved into his personal space, leaving nowhere for Ian to hide.

"I know you don't believe me, but I will prove it to you. I will work hard to prove it to you. I came here for the chance to win you back, to make right what I got wrong all those years ago."

Ian met his gaze head on. "I'd like to see you try."

Jessen's bright smile returned. "Watch me earn you, Ian. I will. I will earn you."

Ian eyed him skeptically. "You're going to live here?"

Jessen nodded.

"And teach? You?"

"I love teaching."

Ian shook his head. "I feel like I'm in the middle of some elaborate joke."

"Funny, I still feel like I'm dreaming."

He knew Jessen was going to kiss him, knew it, but Ian wasn't prepared.

It stole his breath and his reason.

Jessen grabbed his face with both hands and claimed him, smashing his mouth down over his and pushing him back until his body jangled the piano's keys.

There was nothing tentative or tepid about it. Jessen's desperation was evident. His hands slipped up into Ian's hair, fisting it, which made Ian moan into the kiss.

The tall blond echoed it, pulling back to change the angle of his attack. Then he was there again. Both hands on Ian's head, tilting it just the way he wanted while he licked into his mouth.

Ian groaned.

God, it was so, so good.

They broke apart, and Jessen rested his forehead against Ian's, his breathing ragged.

"*Faen, I* shouldn't have done that. It's too soon," he babbled. "Fuck, I'm so sorry."

Ian knew he was right, they still had a lot to work through, but...he'd missed him. Missed his taste and his scent, the feel of him. His music. His very soul.

"Jessen..."

"Yeah?" So much hope in those brilliant, blue eyes.

"Don't stop kissing me."

Jessen smiled. A smile so bright it nearly banished the shadows between them. He ran his knuckles gently over Ian's cheek, searching his eyes before zeroing in on his mouth.

"Never, young Ian. Never."

Chapter 14

Jessen

We're skipping ahead again, but I can't seem to stop myself. Having my hands on Ian Waters after such a long, long drought is overwhelming in every sense.

There's so much I want to tell him. So much I need to apologize for, atone for. But mostly I just need him. And I'm angry that I denied myself this with him for so long.

He's kissing me, letting me kiss him, and I can tell he's still pissed. He has every right to be. He's biting my lip a little too hard, and it shouldn't turn me on. God, but it does.

He wants to punish me. I want to let him. I need absolution.

I need him.

"Ian..."

He has dropped his head to my shoulder and is breathing hard, gripping the front of my shirt like he's worried he might keel over. I can relate.

I'm trembling. He's always had this effect on me, but right now I'm scared. I don't want to fuck this up. Again.

"Ian." I slide my fingers into his hair, massage his scalp, tend to him.

He's breathing and shaking and muttering. When he looks up at me, his eyes shimmer with tears that refuse to fall.

"Baby…"

I kiss him again, tasting salt and hope and need. It's softer but no less intense. We're sort of dancing around what we want, what we both want.

What he needs, what I need.

Releasing him, I stand and cross to the window. I pull down the shade. Moving to the door, I lock it.

I can feel Ian's eyes on me, the moss-green eyes I've dreamt of every damn night.

I'd looked for him in others. Tried to replace him and thought I had a few times, only to wake to bitter disappointment and the inevitable self-loathing that came with morning-afters.

There's only ever been him for me, and there only ever will be. I knew it the moment we met, even though I eventually lied to myself and convinced myself he was better off without me. That I was destined for a life on the road with my brother.

Sex, drugs, rock and roll. No ties. No tethers. No responsibilities.

Mattias had always made it sound so appealing.

The reality was a cold-hearted bitch, and she wasn't mine to tame. I'd left my heart in Philadelphia. And right now he's looking at me like he wants to kill me. Or eat me. Or both.

I want both.

I lean against the door, and we just stare at each other.

Ian is so beautiful it makes my soul ache.

For all these years, I've been picturing the tall, lanky teen with thick, dirty blond hair and ridiculously long eyelashes. And that mouth, that wide, full mouth that always looks like he's just finished eating ripe cherries. His lips are a deep, vibrant red that just invites you to nibble and suck.

And, God, his tongue is a menace.

I'd only let him go down on me once back then because that one time had threatened my sanity. He was so young and so inexperienced, and so everything he'd done had been by instinct. And his instinct, apparently, was to drive me mad.

His nostrils flare, and my heart is rattling around in my ribcage. I don't want to break the silence. I've said I was sorry a few times since he got here, but I know the words aren't ever going to be enough.

He has no proof I mean anything I'm saying, so I don't blame him for the look he's giving me now. Part lust and part loathing.

I take a shuddering breath.

Ian smiles, but it isn't friendly.

"Take off your clothes."

My eyelids flutter because...*fy faen*...

I toe off my shoes and peel off my socks, dropping them by the door. Then I stand and grab the hem of my tee, ripping it off. It lands on the floor.

Ian is watching me like I'm prey. He licks his lips, and my movements falter. Hand on my buckle, I can't stop looking at his mouth.

"Why did you stop?" He asks, his eyes locked on my fly.

I'm hard already. Christ, I have been since he walked into the room. Playing guitar when you're sporting a boner isn't fun, but I'd gladly suffer for him. I'd do anything for him, if he only knew.

"Come here."

I obey immediately and am in front of him in seconds.

He grabs roughly at my belt and wrenches it open, the buckle obscenely loud in the room. Ian pops the button of my fly and lowers the zipper.

There's immediate relief for my aching cock, and I am grateful. The reprieve doesn't last for long. Without preamble, Ian wraps his hand around my flesh and tugs it out, straight into his mouth.

I cry out because...because...*Jesus*... "Ian," I croak.

He sucks me, licks around my cockhead greedily before releasing me and pushing me back a few steps.

"I told you to take your clothes off."

"Baby..."

"Don't *baby* me. I'm not done looking at you."

I don't hesitate anymore. I shove my jeans and my boxers to my ankles and step out of them, kicking them aside.

"Fuck," he breathes while I stand there, more exposed than I have ever been in my life. His eyes drift up to mine, and I literally gasp.

Whatever he needs to tell himself, to tell me, I know he loves me. Or could again.

Ian Waters is everything good in this world. He's kind and loyal, dedicated, and intelligent beyond belief. He's been kicked, dragged, broken, and left behind. And I've contributed to that.

No more.

All I want to do is slip him underneath my ribs and keep him safe from whatever might harm him. I want his smile back. I miss his laughter. I need his love. He improves me. Makes me want to be a better version of myself. Not for him, but for me.

And I walked away. Fucking idiot that I am.

"Did you think of me at all?"

"Every fucking day," I tell him because it's true.

He's staring at my dick, which twitches and dances under his gaze. I want him so bad, need him so much.

"There was a period when I thought I'd made you up," he says, his gaze drifting up to mine. "When I was about eight years old, they told my parents I had ADD. They put me on some meds that fucked with my brain chemistry. I had horrible nightmares, vivid waking dreams. One of my teachers spoke with social services, since I was in the system already, and they stepped in to have me re-evaluated. That's when they declared me a genius and put me in a different school.

"But those waking dreams, they were so real to me. And most of them were…brilliant. Beautiful. When you left, I almost convinced myself you were one of them."

"You asked me if I were real."

He nods.

"I wasn't, but I wanted to be. I am now. I'm here."

He bites his lip. "For how long?"

I hold out my hands. "For as long as you will have me."

Ian lunges forward and drops to his knees in front of me, takes me into his mouth and sucks me in until I hit the back of his throat.

It's brutal, and I have to hold onto his shoulders to keep from falling over. I'm so close to coming, my legs shake.

This is worship. He's worshiping me, and it should be the other way around.

I cup his shoulders in my hands and ease him off me.

Ian looks up at me, lips swollen and eyes puffy with tears streaming down his cheeks. He's wrecked. He's wrecking me.

I kneel and reach for my pants.

Ian's eyes widen with panic, but narrow when I pull out my wallet. I've been walking around with a condom and a little packet of lube since I last saw him.

Wishful thinking? Perhaps, but here we are.

He watches me palm them and then I'm back in front of him. Both of us on our knees. Both terrified.

I drop the stuff on the bench and reach for him.

Ian lifts his arms when I finger the hem of his tee.

I want to cry.

"I love you," I say, because I can't keep it in any longer. He doesn't reply as I set his shirt aside, just sits down and stretches out his legs, giving me access to his belt. I strip him.

God in Heaven, he is glorious. Creamy, golden skin and legs for days.

"You don't even work out, do you?"

He blinks slowly, a little grin curving the side of his mouth.

I lean down and lick his abs, and Ian gasps. He flattens himself on the scratchy carpeting and just…surrenders to me. His trust in me is mindblowing, but I'm more interested in blowing his mind.

I straddle his thighs and brace myself on my hands over him, staring down into that beautiful face.

His hands knead my thighs. Gently, tentatively. All of the fire of only moments ago is gone, replaced by something else.

When I lean down and kiss him, he sighs. A little hiccupping sound that wrenches my heart. I hurt my boy, my baby. I hurt him so deeply.

I pour every apology I can into the kiss, and he drinks them down, sighing against my lips. I kiss his eyelids, his cheeks, his chin, that mouth. I work my way down his throat to his pecs, his abs. Lower.

His cock dances under me and mine is spilling pre-come all over his thigh. I lick him, and he shudders. Sucking him into my mouth, I work him gently. His dick pulses against my tongue and I moan around him.

"Jessen…"

Just the sound of my name on his lips, uttered in that breathy, needy voice, has me on the verge of orgasm.

I can't wait any longer. I grab the lube.

Ian's gaze flicks down to his legs where I have all but pinned them with my weight. He looks back up at me, confused.

I open the packet and coat two of my fingers. Lifting off him a little, I reach back and touch myself, flinching when the cold hits my heat.

He gasps.

"What are you doing?" He sounds awestruck.

"I've thought of little else for seven years, Ian. Please tell me I can have this, even if I don't deserve it."

"You can have anything you want."

I have to close my eyes. This man.

This man.

One finger is easy, my body welcomes it. I rock into the building pleasure. Two fingers is a bit of a stretch. I open my eyes to find Ian watching me intently.

"Why won't you let me do that?"

"You want to?"

"Yes," he answers before I can finish asking. I hand him the lube.

Ian sits up, taking it and coating his fingers as I had done. He wraps one arm around my waist, and our faces are a breath apart. He stares into my eyes and reaches around me, slipping his fingers alongside mine.

I remove one, he adds one, and we're both inside me.

It's insanely hot.

I can't look into his eyes because it's too intense, so I focus on his mouth.

He keeps licking his lips, biting the tip of his tongue.

"I've never..."

"Neither have I."

His gaze locks with mine. "You've never...been fucked?"

I shake my head.

I want to tell him I've been saving myself for him, but that's not entirely accurate. The thing is, I've always been his. And giving myself to anyone else like this, whether I ever saw him again or not, seemed...wrong. It wasn't for a lack of trying. I just couldn't do it.

But he'd think I was making it up, trying to win him back.

The simple truth is Ian Waters ruined me for anyone else.

He surprises me by kissing me. It's so sweet I unravel.

Between us, we have three fingers inside me. I stretch while Ian strokes, and it's maddeningly delicious.

I break the kiss and drop my head to his shoulder, my hips starting to move on their own.

"You want me inside you?"

I nod against his warm skin.

"Lift up."

I do.

We remove our fingers and I feel empty. Bereft. But Ian is ripping open the condom, slipping it on, and then he's there.

"Let me in," he whispers.

His cockhead breaches me, and I gasp, shuddering.

"I've got you. I'll take care of you," he says, his hand on my back. His breath in my ear.

He plants little kisses on my neck and shoulder and I just grab his shoulders and hang on.

I feel him splitting me open, and it's like nothing I've ever experienced. There's pain, yes, but it's a dull echo in some far off chamber. I'm too amped up just to be here with him, too overwhelmed with love and gratitude to feel anything more.

We ease into it.

He pets and soothes me, I lower incrementally until I'm fully seated on him. It's like being rendered in two but from the inside. I'm full and uncomfortable, and yet I never want to leave this spot. It's the closest I've ever been to Ian. To anybody.

I'm so glad it's him.

I'm so fucking glad.

I raise my head and meet his gaze. He looks awestruck.

"I never thought I'd see you again, much less…this."

"Thank you," I say. "Thank you for…just thank you."

"Jessen. Move."

When I do we both groan.

I cup his cheek, nip at his mouth, and he opens for me.

I open for him, slowly. Surely. Every stroke feels better than the last, and soon I am riding him properly. My ass is burning.

The carpet burns the skin of my kneecaps. I'm going to feel both tomorrow. Right now, I couldn't care less.

He breaks away and falls onto his back. I follow him down, attacking his neck while I find a rhythm.

"Fuck…Jessen…"

I have no words. I didn't know it would be like this. That we could be us again. Hoped, maybe, but never truly believed. He amazes me. I am amazed.

His hands slide into my hair, and he pulls my face to his. The kisses are uncoordinated, and my pace is unsteady. None of it matters. All that matters is us. Here. Now.

I bear down on him, and he moans.

"Oh fuck, oh fuck…oh fuck." He repeats the mantra over and over, getting quieter each time.

I change the angle a bit and the knob of his cock rakes over my prostate. I yell.

"Fuck, yes," he growls, grabbing my hips.

I feel him bend his knees behind me and then he's thrusting up, rutting into me. Ian's face is a mask of determination. His eyes are locked on mine.

"Fuck, Jessen, fucking come. I'm not…I can't…I…"

He wraps his hand around my cock and immediately sets a brutal pace. I'm overstimulated. I can't control myself.

I feel him pulse inside me, see his eyes close, watch his mouth form a perfect O as his grip on me tightens, and I'm coming.

I'm flying.

I'm soaring.

He's screaming my name, and I'm whispering his like a prayer.

Ian…Ian…Ian…

Acknowledgments

Big thank you to Mr. X for encouraging me to pursue my dreams, even if they are a little bent.

Thank yous also go to the XiPs for their continued support. I have the best readers in the world!

As always, I have to thank my network which includes Susan Scott Shelley, Veronica Forand, Roan Parrish, Avery Flynn, and so many more talented authors.

Also by Xio

When Frankie Meets Johnny

Scottish ex-pat Frankie Llewellyn lives and breathes music. Working late nights at WKMP, a radio station in suburban Philadelphia, he can play what he wants, sleep in every morning, and no one gives him any grief. No one but his most recent ex-boyfriend. Frankie is a serial monogamist, but after this latest break-up, he's worried he'll end up alone with nothing but his records to keep him warm at night.

When the station hires someone to do some much-needed renovations, Frankie is horrified to find out the work will be done during his overnight shift. But it makes the most sense, so he's resolved to take one for the team. After he meets the mysterious contractor, a gorgeous, lumberjack of a man named John Burton, Frankie decides it may not be such a hardship after all.

John is reserved, and a bit mysterious. Quite the contrast to Frankie's drama-filled life. But, as their friendship grows, John's quiet presence has Frankie singing a new song.

About the Author

Xio Axelrod is a USA Today bestselling author of love stories, contemporary romance and (what she likes to call) strange, twisted tales.

Xio grew up in the music industry and began recording at a young age. When she isn't writing stories, she can be found in the studio, writing songs, or performing on international stages (under a different, not-so-secret name). She lives in Philadelphia with one full-time, indoor husband and several part-time, outdoor cats.

Where to find Xio…
www.xioaxelrod.com
xio@xioaxelrod.com

www.ingramcontent.com/pod-product-compliance
Lightning Source LLC
Chambersburg PA
CBHW052010170626
46808CB00007B/2855